the Lure

the
Lure

Lynne Ewing

BALZER + BRAY

An Imprint of HarperCollins*Publishers*

Balzer + Bray is an imprint of HarperCollins Publishers.

The Lure

Copyright © 2014 by Lynne Ewing

All rights reserved. Printed in the United States of America.

No part of this book may be used or reproduced in any manner whatsoever without written permission except in the case of brief quotations embodied in critical articles and reviews. For information address HarperCollins Children's Books, a division of HarperCollins Publishers, 10 East 53rd Street, New York, NY 10022.

www.epicreads.com

ISBN 978-0-06-220688-6

Library of Congress Control Number: 2013951698

Typography by Ray Shappell

13 14 15 16 17   LP/RRDH   10 9 8 7 6 5 4 3 2 1

First Edition

For Alessandra Balzer

the LURE

For Angela,
With love and best
wishes,
Lynne Ewing

1

The night heat melted over me, the quiet unsettling since the laughter had stopped. I leaned against a tree pocked with bullet holes and scanned the row houses across the street—pretty homes, once, which the owners had padlocked and left to rot.

"They shot out the streetlight," Ariel said, easing next to me, her breath sweet from drinking at Omar's party. "Do you think they know we're here?"

"They'd be chasing us if they did," I whispered.

From the opposite direction, a rusted station wagon turned the corner and rattled toward us, the headlights beaming across the weeds before sweeping over three homeless teens who lounged on a stoop. Smoke hazed around the first boy, who sucked on something cupped in his hand. I recognized the oldest, his long hair matted. He'd come after us before. The skinny guy next to him shook a beer before he popped the tab. A fine mist sprayed over all three as the car passed and darkness concealed them again.

Ariel glanced back at Kaylee and Melissa, who straggled behind us, their pace slowed to avoid tripping over the tree roots that had broken through the sidewalk. "Kaylee drank too much," Ariel said. "We'll never be able to sneak her past those guys."

"Go back and tell Melissa to get her moving the other way. I'll stay."

Ariel didn't argue. Tonight was my turn. She crept through the weeds, her tight jeans gathering burs as thorned branches caught in her long hair, which was naturally dark brown but had been dyed reddish blond.

I unzipped my purse and grasped the hammer inside. The steel handle, smooth and easy in my fist, gave me a sense of control.

Another car turned onto the street, farther away than the first. I waited for the headlights to lift the shadows, but the car was driving dark.

Adrenaline shot through me. I hurled a stone at Ariel but hit a clump of crabgrass, scattering moths without getting her attention.

My stomach tightened. I had already learned that there were worse things in life than dying. I threw myself into a run, taking a chance that the guys on the stoop had also seen the car and were hiding. Too often, in the Borderlands, the homeless dopers became target practice.

My legs thrashed through the chickweed, raising a storm of gnats, before my feet came down hard on the broken brick walk, the insides of my tennis shoes grinding at my blisters.

Ariel looked up, surprised to see me sprinting toward her. I pointed to the street and motioned for her to get down. She peered through the scrim of leaves, saw the car, and dropped. Kaylee fell beside her and lowered her head below the weeds as Melissa spread out flat on the nettles. I slid next to Kaylee, squishing into the blackened leaves, the smell of brackish water and slime mold rising from the drainage ditch.

"Lord Jesus . . ." Kaylee began.

I silenced her with a nudge.

The car, packed with gangsters, rolled past us, gun barrels thrust from the windows, Lobos inside, dressed for a mission: black knit caps pulled down to their eyebrows, the necks of their white T-shirts up over the lower half of their faces, leaving only their eyes exposed.

"They're gunning for Rico," Ariel whispered, her hoop earrings tangling in her curls. "He's been *puto*-ing out their graffiti."

"How do you know?" I asked in a low voice.

"I watched him," Ariel said. Sometimes, she went tagging with Rico and, while he defaced the Lobos' *placas* and left a challenge with his name, Ariel sprayed the walls with bright-colored murals that no one crossed out because everyone loved her wild style.

I placed the hammer back in my purse, took out the cell phone that belonged to Rico, and texted, *Lobos R after U!*

When the g-car swung left toward the projects, I gave the phone to Kaylee, who immediately understood and punched in her home number. "Lobos are coming," she said, her words slurred by alcohol. She handed the phone back to me, her icy fingers barely able to hold it. "Rico's got to stop before he gets us all killed."

Gunfire shattered the night. The blasts echoed and reechoed

nearby, the firepower cracking harder than thunder. Kaylee flinched but I barely reacted to the noise anymore.

When the barrage ended, I waited for return fire. None came.

Melissa looked at me. "It sounded like they were shooting up the vacant buildings. Why would they waste bullets?"

"They didn't," Ariel replied before I could. "They were after Rico."

"That's too crazy, even for Rico," Kaylee said. "He wouldn't try to outrun them, would he, Blaise?"

"He might," I whispered, my stomach queasy. I had seen what bullets could do to a friend. In seventh grade, a drive-by had killed my best friend Gabriella while we were walking home from school. I had screamed her name while the drug dealer who had been the real target fired at the car, his bullets punching the air above us as Gabriella's blood gushed over me.

The *vroom* of a car engine startled me back to the present. I lifted my head as the g-car took the corner, headlights on now that the mission was completed. Tires shrieked in a sideways skid and rubber scorched the pavement. The gangsters inside uncovered their faces. I recognized all of them from my high school. Hard-core Lobos who called their crew the *locos*, which meant "the crazy ones." In street language, it also meant "the brave ones." Killing Rico would earn them the right to that name forever. In the back-seat, the only girl, Gatita, took off her knit cap and let her hair flow into the breeze.

My phone beeped. Rico had texted, *M Ok. U?*

I sent back a smiley face and finally exhaled. "Rico's okay,"

I announced as I slipped the phone deep in the pocket of my baggy jeans.

"You have to be careful, Blaise," Ariel said. "If Rico keeps this up, Lobos are going to come after you and Satch."

I said nothing. I already knew that being one of Rico's best friends made me a target.

"Anyway, Lobos aren't the danger now," Ariel said. "We have to get out of here before those dopers come after us." She pulled herself up and, keeping low, crept away through the weeds that lined the drainage ditch, Melissa close behind her.

Kaylee giggled and lolled back into the grass. "My legs aren't working."

"Try again." I stood and grabbed her arm. "And don't do this to be funny."

"I'm not," she squealed as loud thudding footsteps came from the dark.

The dopers smashed over the sweetbriar and ran toward us, their voices filled with an ugly excitement that caused my skin to prickle.

"We got them!" the first one shouted. He carried a rope, coiled around his dirt-caked arm.

The scrawny teen hurled a beer can at us, then a stone, his eyes wild as he picked up a broken bottle. "Don't run. We just want to party."

"We'll be nice," yelled the one who had chased us through the Borderlands less than two weeks ago. He wiped at the mangy brown hair that fell across his face.

"Help me," Kaylee whimpered.

"I'm trying." I tugged on her arm, but she weighed more than my 103 pounds, and I couldn't lift her alone.

Ariel spun around and raced back to us. "On the count of three!" she shouted, seizing Kaylee's free arm. "One. Two. Three!"

We yanked Kaylee to her feet and ran with her tottering between us, through the drainage ditch and onto the street, where the light stretched our shadows into long silhouettes in front of us.

"No one will ever find our bodies," Kaylee moaned.

"Stop it," Ariel snapped at her. "Just run."

Already the shadows of the guys chasing us bobbed into my side vision, their sour odor infusing the heat.

Still sprinting, I released my hold on Kaylee and pulled out the hammer, confident that I could stop one guy, maybe two. I only needed to slow them until Kaylee and Ariel got farther away.

I started to turn back when Melissa, a block ahead of us, shouted, "Cops!"

Three squad cars, one after the other, chased through the intersection near her, their sirens blaring with high-tech blasts, bar lights flashing over trees and an abandoned car.

In the same moment, the steps behind us fell silent. Like phantoms, the guys chasing us had disappeared, probably slithering into crawl spaces and basements in the abandoned homes, where cops would never find them.

Kaylee grabbed her side and, bending over, gasped for air.

"Come on. You know they'll be back." I pulled her forward, my own feet burning with pain.

We crossed the intersection and, after two more blocks of

running in the steamy heat, we left the Borderlands, a stretch of city blocks that separated the neighborhoods of three rival gangs. Mass 5, Lobos, and Core 9. This was a part of Washington, D.C., that no tourist ever saw.

Ariel smiled and pinched her false eyelashes, which were peeling off at the edges. She wore heavy black eyeliner in wings to the sides of her brown eyes. "We survived another night," she said.

"Sun hasn't come up yet," I countered as we entered the alley behind Mr. Tulley's liquor store that marked the beginning of our neighborhood.

Melissa scooped up her shiny black hair and held it on top of her head to cool off. She wore a guy's T-shirt that she'd cut down to a sleeveless, slinky top that revealed her flat stomach above her hip-hugging jeans. She started singing, the way she did when she was happy. "Did anyone talk to Trek before we left the party?" she asked finally.

"Why?" Kaylee said, swaying slightly.

When Kaylee grabbed the fence to steady herself, Mr. Tulley's Doberman charged from his wooden crate and launched himself against the wire mesh, startling us with his barking. We squealed and jammed against each other, our yells exciting the dog, whose growls became vicious.

Laughing, her voice raised over the barking, Melissa said, "I don't know. I thought he might have said something about me."

"Someone's crushing," Ariel teased.

"Whatever." Melissa smiled, showing off her dimples and perfect teeth. Tall and curvy, with delicate features, she had green eyes that radiated joy and the promise of fun. Everything about her was flawless, except for her hands, which were red and chapped, the fingernails torn to the quick. During the winter, I gave her my gloves and went without.

"I'm going after Trek," she said. "He's got money and looks and—"

"That stupid dog!" Kaylee interrupted, anger twisting her pretty face.

"It's just a dog," I said as we reached the end of the alley, where layers of graffiti crisscrossed the garage doors. "What's wrong with you?"

"Nothing's wrong," she said, but her voice sounded strange.

Melissa started singing again, strolling ahead of us.

"Would you please stop?" Kaylee snapped. "You're giving me a headache."

Melissa swung back, the truth dawning. "If you staked out Trek, I'll back off. I saw you with him, but I didn't think it was more than talk."

"I hate Trek," Kaylee replied. "How can you think I'd want him? He's conceited and cruel and . . ." She stopped when she realized we were staring at her. "He's a monster."

"Everyone likes him, Kaylee," Ariel said defensively.

"He's always a gentleman with me," Melissa added. "He knows how to treat a girl right."

Kaylee stopped in front of the Laundromat where we normally said our good-byes, her fingers tapping out her aggravation on the shopping cart that belonged to Miss Beverly, who stood inside while a washer spun her only clothes.

"You're living in the wrong neighborhood if you're looking for Prince Charming," Kaylee said to Melissa. "And you're a fool to think you're going to find him here." Staggering, she walked away.

"She's wasted," Melissa said. "Why'd she drink so much?"

"Why do any of us drink?" Ariel said.

"I better follow her and make sure she gets home." I left them and found Kaylee in front of my grandmother's church, kicking at the white dandelion heads that dotted the lawn. She twirled unsteadily through the floating seeds until they spun with her, then she flicked on a fancy butane lighter and set fire to the tiny swirling parachutes. A row of feathery seeds flashed into flame and settled in her brown hair.

"Kaylee!" I patted out the fire, the stench of singed hair wafting between us, then took the silver lighter that she'd stolen from someone at the party and tossed it in the gutter. "What happened tonight, Kaylee?" I asked. "You're acting crazy."

Kaylee stared at her blackened thumbnail as we started down the street. "Trek said Core 9 has been courting you. Why didn't you tell me?"

"I was waiting until I'd made up my mind." I tried to keep my pride from showing, but we both knew I was the lucky one, the one chosen. Our neighborhood crew didn't accept just anyone who wanted to join. You had to have something to give. And I never backed down from a fight.

"Did Trek ask you?"

"The 3Ts did." That alone gave me prestige. Everyone feared Tara, Tanya, and Twyla, who were Core 9 homegirls.

As we turned the corner, Kaylee slowed her pace. The squad

cars that had passed us earlier blocked the street near Orchid Terrace, a huge complex built of gray cinderblocks where she lived with her mother and sisters, and eighty-nine other poor families.

People in bathrobes and pajamas had gathered to watch the police officers cordon off the wasteland of vacant buildings. Yellow crime scene tape wagged in front of Rico's mother, who stood beside the officer in charge. She pointed to the bullet-pitted plywood that covered a window, probably where she had last seen Rico. She didn't know yet that he was safe, and I couldn't tell her, because the cops would start questioning me.

Kaylee opened the door to Orchid Terrace and, without saying good-bye, headed inside.

I caught the door before it closed. "Is this how it's going to be?"

She turned too quickly and fell against the wall. "Why prolong it?" she asked angrily. "You're going to leave me behind just like Trek said you would."

"I haven't decided yet," I said, wondering why Trek had told Kaylee about all of this when he had just met her at the party. Maybe he'd wanted to impress her.

"You'll say yes, like Melissa and Ariel already have." Her face puckered. "You should have told me about them, too."

"Nothing's going to affect our friendship," I promised.

"We'll see." She gave me a sad smile and, teetering against the wall, walked away.

That deep, aching sadness, always inside me, stirred closer to the surface. I started running and didn't stop again until I lifted the door to the garage behind my grandmother's house. I eased inside, next to her '89 Chevy. My grandmother rode the bus to work, even though she worked the graveyard shift, and saved her car to drive to church and, at times, to visit my dad at the cemetery. On those days, I pretended not to hear her when she asked me if I wanted to come along.

I unlocked the door to the kitchen and went inside, the hot air thick with camphor and eucalyptus from my grandmother's arthritis rubs. The green linoleum crackled as I crossed to the living room and switched off the lamp that she always left on for me when she went to work. The sudden darkness would tell anyone watching the house that I had come home, but I didn't want to be an easy target for a drive-by either.

Using the streetlight that shone through the window, I turned on the burner beneath the teakettle. Blue flames shot up with a loud pop and the smell of gas leaked into the room.

While I waited for the water to boil, I opened the refrigerator—I'd removed the bulb months ago so no shooter could catch my silhouette—and grabbed the milk carton, which had been almost empty this morning. It was half-full now. My grandmother had added water to stretch the milk.

I slammed the refrigerator, grabbed the packets of condiments that I'd taken from the food court on my last field trip to the Smithsonian, and tore open four. After squeezing ketchup into my cup, I added hot water and stirred, then leaned against the counter and sipped the sweet-and-sour ketchup soup as an odd feeling came over me.

I glanced up. A shadow rushed across the living room.

Setting the cup aside, I took the hammer from my purse and crept forward.

Through the barred window, I saw only my grandmother's rosebushes, the dewy petals glistening in the moonlight, but the quiet creak of the porch steps told me someone was coming to the door. I stole over to the entrance and watched the doorknob turn.

2

The view through the peephole was completely black. Whoever stood on the porch had covered the hole with their hand so I couldn't see out. I placed my palm flat against the door and felt the slight movement of someone pressing to test the hinges and deadbolts. Maybe peewees were trying to find an open house to burglarize, or the homeless guys from the Borderlands had followed me after all. But then, I thought about the Lobos I'd seen tonight. Maybe they'd grown tired of gunning for Rico. I jerked my hand back, annoyed, and suppressed the desire to open the door and smash in someone's face in case a crew of Lobos stood on the porch, weapons ready to fire.

I slid the phone from my pocket and called Satch, who lived in the row house at the opposite end of the block with his aunt.

"Someone's trying to break in," I said in a low voice.

"I'll come through the passage," he said quickly.

Years ago, his dad had broken through the attic walls to make a secret passageway between the adjacent row houses. He had planned to use it for his escape on the inevitable day when the police came for him. But when that day arrived, Satch had been home and his dad hadn't wanted his son to see him turn coward and run. He was now serving three consecutive life sentences in a Colorado supermax.

During his trial, the media had called him scum, but his homeboys had called him T-Rex. After they had beaten Satch into Core 9, they'd called him Baby Rex—a street name he hated, so Rico and I never used it. But that name was no worse than the one that Trek had tried to give him: Lost Boy. Satch had run away the day the cops arrested his dad. *Lost Boy* flyers had appeared on lampposts overnight.

Slipping the phone back in my pocket, I hurried up to the second floor, turned down the narrow hallway that ran alongside the stairs, and pulled on the rope attached to the trap door in the ceiling. The ladder unfolded and clattered down, bringing a wave of stale air and attic dust. It landed with a boom that shook the house.

Within seconds, footsteps pounded overhead and a bobbing light appeared in the hatch. Satch climbed down the ladder, bare-chested, wearing jeans, the beam from his flashlight streaking across the walls.

He snapped off the flashlight and clasped my elbow. "Where?"

"Front door," I said.

He pushed around the ladder, his six-foot-three body brushing against mine, and made his way to the top of the stairs, then down to the living room. He crossed to the window, his stride fluid, his strength showing in the way he carried himself. I watched him peer outside, his handsome face, without scars, still perfectly shaped, because when he fought, he always won. In his left earlobe, he wore the diamond that had belonged to his father. His chest bore a single tattoo, *Chantelle*, his mother's name, that Rico had punctured into his skin using a straight pin and pen ink after her funeral, when Satch was ten.

Judging from the way Satch opened the front door, he hadn't seen anyone outside. He walked onto the porch, kicked at a rope left on the top step, and continued into the yard, where he shined the flashlight over the vent openings to the crawl space beneath the house before he inspected the cubby under the stoop where my grandmother stored her gardening tools.

Finally, he gave me the smile that the girls at school adored, his expression a mix of teddy-bear brown eyes and chiseled features. "Hey, Toughness, they're gone."

His use of my nickname reminded me that we hadn't always been friends. When I was younger, I had been afraid of Satch. Most kids were and, like me, they weren't allowed to play with him because of his dad. But after losing Gabriella, something inside me had shifted and the next time I saw Satch, I hadn't run. I had stared at him, lifting my chin in defiance. My challenge had made him laugh, until he had realized I was the girl who had just watched her friend die. Then, the compassion in his eyes had brought tears to mine. To my utter surprise, he had held me and, after that, called me Toughness for having had the courage to face him.

"Why are you just standing there?" Satch asked, pulling me back to the present. "It's safe to come out now."

I set my hammer on the porch and walked toward Satch, the night breeze velvet on my skin.

"Thanks for coming over." I snapped a leaf off the sassafras tree and breathed in its root beer and licorice aroma before I held the rounded lobes up to the sky.

"What are you looking at?" Satch eased closer behind me.

"The color of the leaf changes," I explained, gazing at the lush moon-fed greenish yellow. "It becomes chartreuse, but . . . otherworldly, not like everyday colors. . . . Do you want to see?"

I turned to give him the leaf and, when I looked up at him, the sadness in his expression startled me. "What's wrong?"

He seemed to shake himself out of it and, turning, looked up at the tree. "Just thinking how I saw that tree every day," he joked, "and never appreciated it until it was too late."

"The tree's not going anywhere." I laughed, tickling the leaf over his chin.

He looked back at me and, when he started to speak, a distant whistle stole my attention. The sweet melody sent a shudder through me.

"Maybe Lobos dropped someone when they drove through our neighborhood," I said.

Sometimes for initiation, Lobos abandoned a new member in enemy territory and left him to kill his way home.

"Easy," Satch said, pulling me behind the tree.

The branches bobbed in front of us as the whistle came again, bringing back the memories of funerals, four in a row. Kids in our neighborhood had used that whistle to locate each other at night until Lobos discovered it and tricked four of our friends into an ambush last summer.

"There." Satch pointed to a maple tree that had grown against a house, its trunk molded into the bricks. From the gloom beneath its branches, a lone figure walked toward us.

I studied the tall silhouette, the easy, athletic stride. "It's Rico," I said as he stepped under the streetlight, his smile as big as the moon.

"*Awooooo,*" Rico howled, like a wolf. "Don't you know Lobos are out? You should be inside."

Satch stepped away from me. "I got love for you, homeboy, but no one wants to hear that whistle again."

"Satch is right," I said, irritated with Rico. "Someday you're going to get shot, fooling around like that."

"I'm Core 9 and I'm going to use that whistle till the day I die." Rico punched Satch's shoulder, then the two clenched hands, leaning into each other before they pulled apart. "I won't let Lobos control my life," Rico said. "They can't kill enough people to make me stop using our whistle."

"You're crazy," Satch said, shaking his head. "What did you do tonight?"

"I gave the Lobos some needed target practice. Bad shots, all of them, they couldn't get a bullet in me."

"Looks like you barely got away." I touched the blood oozing out of the cut on his cheek. "You got to stop."

Some homies craved the danger and gambled their lives, taking risks, because the heavy doses of adrenaline could make them feel as high as an injection of morphine.

"Ariel said the Lobos are gunning for you because you've been messing with their graffiti, again."

Rico shrugged, though his eyes remained tense, as if he still expected an attack. "I cleaned up some walls in their neighborhood."

He glanced at Satch and a look passed between them that I didn't understand. They had been friends since preschool and, by the time they were eight, had started picking up jobs together, sometimes carrying drugs and money for Satch's dad, pulling a red wagon filled with contraband and toys, right past the cops. They went from baby homies to li'l homies and, the summer they turned twelve, they were beaten into Core 9.

Satch pulled his gaze away from Rico and said to me, "I've got to bail. My aunt needs me."

To do what? I wanted to ask. His aunt wasn't even up this late at night, but I didn't call him on his lie.

He flicked on his flashlight and ambled away, the beam squiggling through the dark as he headed home.

"I don't understand what's up with Satch lately," I said to Rico, who was pulling me into his arms.

"It's nothing," Rico replied. "He's moody."

"Only around me," I whispered.

"Stop worrying about it." Rico pressed against me, his breath soft on my face, his clothes smelling of the sultry night. "Think about us instead."

I was the only girl at school who didn't snap to it for Rico. My friends thought I was crazy not to want him, but our homeboys never stopped at kisses and I wasn't ready for babies. Maybe I never would be. In this neighborhood, even toddlers got shot. Besides, I'd watched the worn-out girls at school who had kids. Nothing aged a girl faster than drooling, pooping, screaming babies.

Rico wanted kids, lots of them. Maybe because he didn't know who his father was. Sometimes I caught him studying the men who sat outside Tulley's, as if he were trying to find his features in theirs.

I touched the scar on his chin. I loved the complexity of his face, the unique color of his eyes, a pale brown, almost golden, that matched the color of his skin. I liked the curious way his nose dipped at the end, the double rows of lashes, thick eyebrows, and his lush, black curls.

He pulled me closer and tried to kiss me, his lips soft on mine.

"Satch is right, you know." I laughed, twirling away from him. "You are crazy."

"For wanting you?" he asked, catching me again.

"I know you, Rico—you ran out in front of the Lobos' car and made yourself a target—"

"I don't make myself a target," he said, his fingers pushing my hair away from my eyes. "They're always after me."

"You're taking stupid risks."

"No risk involved. I knew I wouldn't die. The night's not pretty enough for dying." He pressed a finger over my mouth to stop my words. "Someday you're going to find out how selfish I've been, and then, you're going to hate me."

"I could never hate you," I said.

"We'll see." He kissed my forehead. "I'll catch you tomorrow at school." His silver Saint Rita's medal glinted on its chain as he raced away.

I went back to the house and lifted my hammer off the step. Though I didn't know who had been on my porch trying to break in, an odd apprehension stayed with me. I hurried inside, locked and bolted the door, and slept with the attic ladder down in case I needed a quick getaway. The hammer lay cradled under the covers, against me, my blisters raw and stinging.

The next morning, after bandaging my blisters, I squeezed into my tennis shoes and clomped down the stairs. On the bottom step, I grabbed the newel post, unable to ignore my anxiety as I glanced out the window. My grandmother stood outside, the leaves on her scrawny rosebushes fluttering around her. Shadows deepened the hollows under her cheekbones and eyes, the contours sharp against the bright sunlight that fell on her forehead. The robe that had fit her at Christmas flapped around her, engulfing her frame. She clipped a rose, her arm snagging on thorns and, moments later, stepped inside, examining the blood on her thorn-bitten wrist.

"You look tired," I said. *Ready to die.* The thought came unbidden as I embraced her.

"I'm not tired." She kissed my cheek, her lips cracked and rough. "A blessed morning like this one gives me strength." She limped away, her gray hair flattened from the scrub cap she wore at the hospital, where she cleaned the floors.

I followed her into the kitchen. An open bottle of aspirin sat on the table, next to her Bible. The plastic pan she used to soak her feet drained in the sink.

She set the rose in a vase and, after washing her hands, counted out her pills and began breaking them in half to make her prescriptions last longer.

"Grandma, you're losing too much weight."

"No, I'm not." She smiled at me and patted her sunken belly, then saw my face and said, "Maybe a little, but it can't be helped. I have to push myself to get all my rooms mopped."

I started to shake cornflakes into a bowl and paused. "What did you eat at work?"

She waved a hand. "I didn't have time to take a break, even though I had to put it on the log that I did."

I left the cereal for her and tore open a packet of sugar. "I wish you didn't have to work."

"I'm thankful I have a job. You should be grateful that I have one, too. Things could be worse."

"There must be enough for us to live on with your social security and the government checks you get for me." I poured the sugar into my mouth.

"The checks I get for you go straight into savings so you can go to college." She snapped another pill in half. "All your teachers say you're smart."

"That was before," I argued. *Before I watched Gabriella die.* After her death, I couldn't study. Words had jumped around the page, impossible to read. My English teacher had sent me to the school grief counselor, who had just made me angrier. Homework

22

no longer made sense. What did grades matter if I wasn't going to live long enough to graduate from high school?

My grandmother's voice pulled me back to the kitchen. She was still talking about what a good student I was. "Even your test scores show you're—"

"Grandma, I'm being shot at, out there," I said, sugar spitting off my tongue. "I have to run and duck to keep from being murdered and you want me to think about school? One day I'm not going to run fast enough, and then you'll have worked yourself to the bone for nothing. You better stop dreaming about college and use that money for food."

"Where's your faith?" She frowned and put her hands to her temples. "Maybe you should go to church with me instead of loafing with your friends on Sundays."

"Why? Bullets kill good people, too. You and I know that's a fact." I regretted my words the moment I saw the look in her eyes. I had meant Gabriella, but she was thinking about my dad.

"Your father was a hero."

"I know." I looked at his pictures, the yellowed, brittle newspaper clippings taped to the wall. His medals, wrapped in velvet, sat in my closet next to the box that held his gun. His death had happened far away, in Afghanistan. I had seen a casket, not his body. Only bits and pieces of him had come home. I still daydreamed that the government had made a mistake and my father would walk through the front door. No fantasy could bring Gabriella back.

"God won't curse me twice," my grandmother muttered. "I

have faith that He only gives us what we can carry." She left the kitchen without taking her medicine.

I trailed after her. "Maybe we could figure out something so you wouldn't have to work as many hours. Can't we at least try?"

"You worry about school. I'll take care of the rest." She gripped the banister and, without giving me a kiss, or even a smile, started up the stairs.

When her bedroom fan switched on, misery settled over me. The conversation had ended. She was going to bed. As a day sleeper, she used the drone from the fan to block outside noise so she could sleep uninterrupted.

In the dust on the coffee table, I wrote *I love you* in case I didn't come back, then left for school, burdened with her unhappiness on top of my own guilt. I had only known my grandmother to stop smiling once before. Normally talkative, she had gone silent, except for occasionally speaking in a muffled voice to someone on the phone. I hadn't understood what I'd done to upset her.

Weeks later, when we had walked into the courtroom, I had feared she was relinquishing me for adoption until I saw the problem: my incredibly beautiful mother, who opened her arms, waiting for me to run to her. The gesture was for the judge, not me. She had never cuddled me. No one had told me that she had been released from her court-ordered rehab, again.

After casting shy, seductive glances at the bailiff and flirting with my grandmother's lawyer, my mother had directed her sultry gaze at the judge, telling him how much she had missed me. She'd practically begged him to let me live with her. She'd wanted full custody.

Even as a little girl I knew that she had only wanted the monthly checks that came with me. Fortunately, she hadn't been able to charm the judge the way she had controlled other men.

My grandmother had smiled again after the hearing, even when she'd told me that she had to find a job. She'd taken a loan against the house in order to pay the lawyer, and the monthly mortgage payment was now more than her social security check brought in.

Abruptly, I stopped thinking about the past and concentrated on the present. I was nearing school. I gathered myself together, mentally getting ready. Appearance was important. I had to have *the look* that told my classmates I was ready to take on anything. Rico called it a form of self-defense.

The moment I stepped on campus, a *clica* of Lobos girls swarmed around me, their bodies crowding against mine as their threats streamed into the muggy air.

"*La muerta* is what we call you in our neighborhood." Gatita leaned so close her hair tickled over my face. "*La difunta*. You're a dead girl."

Ignoring her, I continued forward, pushing my way past girls who wore the same school uniform as I did—gray skirt, white blouse, and gray sweater—but still found ways to flaunt their gang allegiance in their woven bracelets, silver rings, and the razor-thin eyebrows arched high on their foreheads.

"The *tiros* are going to get you." Gatita pointed her index finger at my temple. "*Pum!* You go with our *puta* enemy Core 9 and we go after you."

The 3Ts had warned me that enemy gang members, especially girls from the Lobos, would try to intimidate me and keep me from joining Core 9.

Gatita kicked my shin and, though the pain felt hot, I smiled.

"*Fue nada, su patada*, little kitty cat," I said, making fun of her gang name while telling her in the best Spanish I could muster that her kick was nothing.

She held up her hand, her fingers splayed to show me the lethal-looking silver rings. The sharp edges on a wolf head glistened in the morning sun. "Maybe you need a scar on your pretty face to match the ones I put on your arm."

Whistles shrilled and two armed security guards raced toward us.

"Snitches get stitches," Gatita warned, slipping her hands into her sweater pockets before she and her homegirls strolled away.

I grinned at the guards, who gave me sour looks before I headed off in the opposite direction, focused on finding my friends.

The 3Ts stood close to the school entrance, watching me, their eyes like stones. Tara started down the steps, Twyla and Tanya behind her. They wore their skirts nine inches shorter than regulation, but the teachers never bothered them about the length.

The other students shifted out of their way, careful around Tara, who liked to fight.

"Hey, Blaise," Tara said, pinching a cigarette from her pocket. A splotch of makeup covered the tattoo on the web between her index finger and thumb, where her homegirls had inked *C9* into her skin. She had to cover it for school so she wouldn't get expelled, but on the street she flaunted it, like I would if I earned mine.

She lit the cigarette, then offered me the first drag, a sign of respect.

I put the cigarette between my lips but didn't inhale. When I handed it back, she said, "What's up with you?"

"Yeah, you should be strutting over the way you handled those girls." Twyla brushed back the purple tendrils clipped into her hair with butterfly barrettes. Her nose, crooked at the end, had scars from her jump-in when she'd joined Core 9.

"I'm worried about my grandmother," I said. "She's working herself to death because of me."

"We've all felt like burdens," Tanya said, her face sympathetic. "Give Tara a yes and after the jump-in, you'll become part of our family. Then, you'll never be alone, and even if something does happen to your grandmother, we'll take care of you."

Tara smiled, sensing my indecision. "I can promise you this," she said, smoke unfurling from her nostrils. "Life gets better when you're ganged up."

At the end of the school day, I hurried out to the curb, where the music from the slow-moving cars battered the heat. Guys riding low in their seats cast brutal glances at their enemies, their faces closing in blank expressions as they drove past the police. I threaded my way through the traffic, the exhaust too noxious to breathe, and joined Melissa, Ariel, and Kaylee, who were waiting for me a block away.

"We're going over to Trek's." Melissa grinned exultantly. "He invited me to his house."

"Then why are *we* going?" I asked, watching Kaylee to see if she was upset. She was smiling a little too broadly for someone who hated Trek.

"The three of you are coming along to make sure I don't do anything stupid," Melissa said as we started walking. "The idea is to bait Trek, not give it all up now."

"It's a bad idea," Kaylee said, running her fingers through her hair. She'd added another streak of red to her bangs, which were almost as long as mine. "Trek's going to be unhappy that we tagged along."

Melissa stopped suddenly. "Don't ruin this for me, Kaylee."

"Me?" Kaylee rolled the word out.

"You trashed him last night," Ariel reminded her as we started forward again.

"I was drunk," Kaylee snapped. "I have the headache to prove it."

"One piece of advice," I said, to break the tension.

Melissa glanced at me. "What?"

"Don't sing," I said.

Ariel snickered. "Seriously, don't even hum."

"I don't see why not," Melissa said. Teasing us, she broke into a love song.

Even Kaylee laughed and shook her head. "That is so totally off-key."

Melissa stopped singing as we neared Trek's home, a narrow, two-story brick house that had no trees in front, only stumps where maple trees had once grown.

Dante stood in the doorway, puffing on a cigarette, trying to look tough, though everyone knew he was on the outs with Trek. When he saw us, he strolled off the porch, his jeans, belted below his hipbones, showing off his paisley boxers. The rutted scar on his cheek wasn't a wound. He had tried to carve *C9* into his skin when he was twelve. He took a long drag and exhaled toward the street. The gesture, as insignificant as a blink, signaled to anyone inside that we looked harmless, no weapons drawn, no danger from guys hiding nearby who were using us as a decoy.

Omar stepped onto the porch. Bulked out with muscles, he seemed even bigger next to Dante, who led us up the front steps and took my purse.

Without greeting me, Omar held his tattooed palms in front of my face. The fingers on his strong hand, the one he used to fire a gun, were callused, which told me he did a lot of dry fire, gun practice without ammunition. He slowly turned his hands to show me that he was going to use the backsides to frisk me. Even so, his touch startled me. I winced as his hands slid over my breasts, into my armpits, and onto my back.

Dante pulled the hammer from my purse, excitement darting into his eyes. "Did you ever use it?"

"Once." The memory still made my stomach clench. A doper had surprised my grandmother in the garage, and when she had refused to let go of her purse, he had knocked her to the ground and stomped on her wrist. Only nine years old, I had grabbed the nearest tool, a hammer, the one I carried with me now. I had swung it at his thigh, then his knee. When he had turned on me, I'd held the hammer with both hands and hit his face.

"You get the hammer back when you leave," Dante said, regarding me with new interest and respect. He placed it on the porch, then motioned Kaylee forward.

"No way," she snapped.

"Kaylee, you promised," Melissa groaned.

"I'm not letting him look in my purse," Kaylee argued.

"Don't start, Kaylee," Ariel warned.

"We're not going to debate it," Omar said indifferently. "Leave if you don't want to be searched."

I didn't glance back to see if Kaylee had left because Omar kneeled in front of me, his face to the side. His hands ran under my skirt, knuckles scraping over my legs, checking for weapons taped to the inside of my thighs.

"Blaise can go in," Omar announced as he stood and began frisking Melissa, who recoiled from his touch.

When Dante opened the front door, I glanced back. Ariel was staring angrily at Kaylee, who stood at the corner, hands on her hips in a defiant stance, her shaggy hair tousled in the wind. My heart dropped. *No, Kaylee.* This was not the time for her antics. She did things on a whim, thinking she was funny, and never considered the consequences. She flashed a cocky grin and turned away as Dante nudged me.

I stepped inside, the brightness in the living room forcing me to squint. Sunlight reflected off the mirrored tabletops, the weapons on the couch, and the glass in the framed pictures of dead homeboys that lined the wall.

From overhead, the clink and jingle of wind chimes caught my attention. Seashells, glass, and metal tubes tied to the upstairs railing swirled and clattered as Trek walked down the stairs, clean-shaven and smelling of soap, his waist-length hair slicked back and held at the nape of his neck. He had no scars, no tattoos, no piercings, and everything I wanted: cars, money, respect, and a big reputation.

His eyes, the blackest I had ever seen, never looked at me.

His gaze danced past me and settled on Melissa, who had just walked inside.

"Hi," she whispered shyly, tilting her head so that her silken hair fell to one side.

Trek kissed her cheek. "Hey, babe." He nuzzled her ear, his arm sliding around her. "Let me get you a beer."

I waited for Ariel, then together we followed Trek and Melissa into the windowless kitchen, where tubs of muscle-building protein powders and vitamins crowded the counter. Trek popped the tabs on two beers and handed one to Melissa, completely ignoring Ariel and me.

"I guess this is how it feels to be part of someone's entourage," I said, bumping awkwardly against Ariel, not sure what to do until I glanced at the back porch and saw two pit bull puppies inside a cardboard box. The smallest popped her white head over the side, her thick paws scratching to get out.

"Puppies," I whispered, prodding Ariel toward the porch. "Look how cute." I picked up the smallest and set her on my shoulder, the puppy's fat belly warm on my neck, her sticky tongue licking my ear.

"Don't get attached," Ariel warned in a hushed tone while scratching the puppy's back. "Trek's probably going to train them to kill."

"He can't. They're too sweet." I set the puppy in with her sister and sat on the floor, resting my hands on the edge of the box, slowly becoming aware of a clicking sound. My stomach clenched as my eyes shot to the corner, where Kaylee sat on a bag of kibble, smiling smugly, snapping the blade of a box cutter in and out of its plastic casing.

"This is so not funny, Kaylee," Ariel hissed, dropping to the floor beside her. "Why did you sneak in?"

"I wasn't going to let those guys touch me," Kaylee said, looking pleased with herself.

I turned to see if Trek had noticed her. He appeared oblivious to anyone but Melissa, who was crowding him against the kitchen counter. She looked down at the floor and smiled too brightly at whatever he was whispering into her ear, then glanced up at him and laughed, her finger gliding over his belt before she pulled back and waited for him to put his arm around her, which he did.

"You're lucky Trek's so into Melissa," I said. "He hasn't seen you."

"I'm sure Trek's into lots of girls," Kaylee smirked.

"Go," Ariel whispered harshly. "Leave. You were stupid to— jeez." Ariel exhaled. "Too late now."

Trek crouched beside me, his hand on my knee. A pleasant shiver raced over me, my body overreacting to the warmth of his fingers on my skin. I glanced at him, but he didn't seem aware that he was touching me. He was grinning at Kaylee, who glared back at him.

"Are you here to return the silver lighter you stole from me last night?" he asked, unruffled. When she didn't reply, he added, "You break into my house and then you mad-dog me like I did something wrong. What's up with that?"

"Maybe I wanted to show my friends that you're not so special."

33

Kaylee stood and walked out, the door slamming behind her and setting off the wind chimes.

I drew in a breath and stared at Ariel, who looked as panicked as I felt, but Trek remained calm.

"Now you see why I need guard dogs?" He laughed before he said to me, "Seems like the dogs got you hooked already. I don't have much time for them. Do you want to earn some extra cash taking care of them for me?"

I did. Of course I did. But that meant going to Trek's house every day, alone. Was I ready for that? I started to make up excuses when the puppies whimpered, their faces nudging against my hands and, to my surprise, I heard myself say, "Sure."

The moment I agreed, Trek's eyes shifted. I had the eerie feeling that he had somehow planned this. I brushed the thought away. What could he want with me when he had Melissa?

He patted my leg. "I'll get Omar to explain the rules about the doors and fix you up with a schedule. No surprise visits," he warned.

As soon as he returned to Melissa, Ariel whispered, "Why wasn't Trek more pissed about Kaylee breaking into his house?"

I looked at the small crescent marks on my knee where his fingernails had dug into my skin. "Maybe he was but didn't show it because of Melissa."

Ariel stared at the door. "How'd Kaylee get inside anyway?"

I shrugged. "The door must have been open."

"We have to drop her," Ariel said. "Seriously."

"She's our friend," I protested.

"That's my point exactly," Ariel said. "She's going to pull us down."

5

Trek named the dogs Skull and Bones, but I called them Pixie and Bonnie. I fed them before school and again in the afternoon, sometimes playing with them through the evening. This morning, Melissa had come with me, her eyes brightening as she told me about all the things that Trek had bought for her. I could smell the newness of her sweater and the tang of her lemon-scented lotion.

"You haven't said anything about my shoes," she said, kicking up her foot.

I glanced at her new designer sneakers. "Pretty," I responded, but my gut reaction told me something was wrong. "Maybe you shouldn't let Trek spend so much money on you."

"Blaise!" She caught my wrist. "Are you jealous?"

"Jealous?" *Was I?* The ache in my chest felt like worry, not envy. "Money makes any guy attractive," I said. "You need to find out what Trek's like when he's not buying you things."

"He's adorable." She laughed and pulled at my skirt. "And you shouldn't be jealous. If you want a guy in your life, all you have to do is fix yourself up. You can't hide your body in clothes that are two sizes too big." She brushed back my bangs. "And you have to get your hair out of your eyes. No one can even see your face."

"Melissa." I batted her hand away. "It just seems like"—*He's trying to buy you!*—"you should go slower."

"Why? My mom knew my dad was *the one* the moment she saw him."

And how long did he stay? Melissa hadn't seen her dad since first grade.

"Relax, Blaise," she whispered as we stepped onto the porch. "I have everything under control. Trek's right where I want him."

In the same moment, Trek opened the door, sunlight falling across his smile. He grabbed Melissa and pulled her, giggling, into the living room while I waited for Omar to frisk me.

I was never going to get used to his hands on me. I stared down at the top of his head, his clean-shaven scalp, ready to jab my knee into his nose if his touch became more than business.

"Okay," he said, standing, his face expressionless. "You can go in."

I smoothed down my skirt and entered the house, pretending not to see Melissa and Trek, who had settled on the couch.

As I headed toward the back porch, with Omar close behind me, the aroma of onions and beef drifted over me. My stomach pinched around the sugar I had eaten for breakfast. I had expected Trek to pay me before now, but the only money I had seen, he had given to Melissa. He probably knew I'd come over twice a day to make sure the puppies were okay even if he never paid me. I felt like they were mine.

In the kitchen, Satch and Rico leaned against the counter, eating steak and cheese sandwiches. Trek was always giving them something extra, even small things like breakfast, because they were his favorites. Rico took risks and Satch was fearless, willing to back up Rico no matter how far he went. Dante sat alone at the small table, his scowl letting me know that he was in trouble with Trek. I glanced up, wondering if he'd accidentally fired a gun again, but I didn't see any new bullet holes in the ceiling.

"Hey, Blaise," Satch greeted me. "Have a sandwich. Trek bought extras."

"I ate already," I said, not wanting anyone to know I was living off packets of ketchup and sugar so my grandmother would eat.

"Blaise." Rico cut in front of Omar and followed me onto the back porch, grease dripping from the wrapper of the sandwich that he held up to me. "Take a bite. Just try it."

He thrust the bread against my lips, our eyes connected, and I wondered if he had recognized the look of hunger on my face. When he was little, his mother hadn't always had enough money to pay a babysitter, so she'd sometimes left him at home alone with only a bowl of cereal while she went to work.

I took a huge bite, letting the mayonnaise and melted cheese run over my lips, my mouth too full to speak.

"Do you want one?" he asked.

I shook my head, smiling. I hated the obligation that came with even small handouts, and I already owed Rico more than I could ever repay.

He went back to the kitchen as I kneeled beside Pixie and

Bonnie, who pawed at the side of their box in greeting before they rolled onto their backs and let me rub their soft bellies.

While I took care of the dogs, Omar, Satch, and Rico talked. They shut Dante out of their conversation and, finally, exasperated with his interruptions, sent him to buy coffees. I tried not to listen to what they were saying, but the name *Danny* kept coming up. Danny had been their friend in elementary school, but living just a few blocks from each other had destined them to become members of enemy gangs. Now they were planning to go after him because he was stealing Trek's customers. I wondered if they had factored Danny's older sister Gatita into their plans. If anything happened to him, her revenge would be unrelenting.

When I'd finished with the dogs, I kissed Pixie on the tip of her nose and breathed in her sweet puppy smell. As I set her in the box with Bonnie, pebbles clinked against the porch window. I froze.

In one graceful move, Omar ducked forward, pulled a Beretta, full-size pistol, from his waistband, and peered out.

"It's Tara." His dark eyes flicked to me. "Come check it out, Blaise. I think she's looking for you."

"Me?"

I glanced at Satch and Rico, who gave me encouraging smiles.

Tara stood in the backyard, near the gate, dressed in her school uniform, her hair in a ponytail that swayed back and forth when she waved for me to join her.

"Call me," Rico yelled before I ran out to the alley where Tara waited for me next to a rusted-out yellow Buick with license plates from New Mexico.

"I thought we should talk alone," Tara said, grinding out her cigarette on the car's bumper. "I want your decision without any influence from your friends."

My heart was thumping so hard, I was afraid she would hear it.

"You're a natural-born fighter, Blaise," Tara said as we started walking toward school. "That's one reason I want you for Core 9. You fight to win. Civilians throw a punch like they're playing tennis, strike and politely wait for a return. They call it fighting fair, but that's the loser's way. You hit fast and keep hitting. I've had my eye on you since you took down Gatita."

"You saw me?"

She nodded. "I know how you got those scars on your arm."

In eighth grade, Gatita had jumped me, trying to steal the cell phone that Rico had given me. Rather than hand it over, I had stuffed it in my bra. I hadn't had time to get out my hammer before her fist came down with a switchblade aimed for my face. I'd swung my arm up to deflect the blow and the razor-sharp edge had sliced my skin. I had kept swinging and, after a dozen more cuts, I caught her wrist and slammed her hand back with such force that she'd stumbled. Stunned more than hurt, she'd run from me.

"You've lived in this neighborhood all your life," Tara continued, "so you know what being a gangster is about. If you have the guts and the strength to be one, and I think you do, then you own the world and everyone in it. Gangsters have the real power, because we don't have to follow the rules."

I said nothing while I thought of my grandmother.

Tara stopped in front of me and placed her hands on my shoulders. "If you want to live your life in a bold and powerful way, do you get a ten-dollar-an-hour job or do you get a gun?"

Tara smiled.

I had made my decision.

6

Later that day, on a field trip to the Smithsonian Museum of Natural History, while Kaylee stared at dinosaur fossils with the rest of our class, I told Melissa and Ariel that Tara had set the date for our jump-in.

"Saturday night," I whispered excitedly. "I can't wait."

Ariel squeezed me against her. "Can you imagine how great we're going to feel when we go back to school on Monday?"

"Everyone is going to step aside," Melissa said softly. "We'll be like celebrities. I wonder if Trek knows."

While Melissa sent a message to Trek, Ariel pulled a mirror from her purse and checked her new lashes. I thought she was smiling at her reflection but, after a minute of watching her primp, I realized she was using the mirror to look behind her.

Curious, I glanced back. Danny leaned against the railing, his school slacks tight over his muscled legs, the cuffs rolled up to show off his hundred-dollar tennis shoes. Only fifteen, he already had a reputation as a hustler, out for the money, and his open-air drug market was stealing Trek's customers. Like most of us, he and Gatita stayed in school so their mom could collect her welfare, but I figured he'd get busted and be expelled before the year was up.

An easy grin crossed his face when he caught Ariel watching him. She snapped her compact closed. "Let's ditch this field trip," she said. "We should be celebrating, not looking at bones."

"I'm for that," Melissa agreed, slowly stepping backward.

We lagged behind the other students and, when our class entered the next hall to view the bones of prehistoric mammals, we took off down the escalator to the exit. Outside, as we waited to cross Constitution Avenue, I looked back. Danny had followed us and stood among the tourists, his gaze fixed on Ariel. His unmasked interest in her scared me. He was attractive, with dark hair and green eyes, a straight nose and square jaw. His homegirls called him *el rompecorazones*, the heartbreaker. But were looks enough to make Ariel cross the line? She couldn't go out with a Lobo without getting herself killed.

I tried to put Danny out of my mind, but by the time we were walking past the Justice Department, I couldn't hold back. "How long has Danny been following you?"

Ariel looked genuinely surprised. "He's in our class. Why do you think he's following me?"

"Get real, Ariel," Melissa said as we crossed Pennsylvania Avenue. "Gatita's probably got you under 24/7 surveillance. Show Blaise what you did."

"There's no way Gatita can know it was me," Ariel said as she took out her cell phone and pulled up a picture. "What was

I supposed to do? She had plastered her name on the back of the community center. She was asking for it."

I stared at the display. On the wall above Gatita's name, in fat neon pink letters, Ariel had sprayed *SCARDY CAT* and, below that, she had drawn a caricature of Gatita, with catlike features, running from three girls with spiked wings and talons for hands, who had clawed *CORE 9* across the wall.

"That is amazing." I laughed, my tension unwinding. Maybe I had misjudged the whole thing.

"I want to show you something else." Ariel slipped her phone away and took out a small velvet bag from which she removed a silver cross that had a loop at the top. "It's called an ankh. It's supposed to protect me."

"Why do you need a charm when you've got Blaise and me to protect you?" Melissa teased.

"It's just I've been thinking that if I could grow up, you know, make it through high school without getting killed, that maybe I could go to California. I saw this show on TV about graffiti artists in Venice Beach and—" She frowned, her gaze focused behind me.

When I looked over my shoulder, Kaylee waved and, grinning, ran toward us.

"I'm not going to hang out with her," Ariel said, stuffing the charm back in its bag. "I can't trust what she'll do."

"Her life is hard," I argued. "She has to take care of her sisters, and her mom can't even get out of bed anymore without Kaylee's help."

"Don't protect her, Blaise," Melissa said. "I'm sorry her mom's sick, but that's no excuse. We all have problems."

Melissa's mom was an alcoholic who worked sporadically in bars. She was hardly ever home.

"I'm tired of making excuses for her," Ariel said.

"Even Trek said we should dump her," Melissa added, easing away from me.

"I'm not going to dump her," I said.

In third grade, Kaylee and I had sworn to be best friends forever. We'd stolen into the church and used the holy water in the stoup to wash out our mouths so our vows would be sacred. Back then, everyone had wanted to be Kaylee's friend. She'd had this energy that could make you feel happy just being around her.

"We'll see you tomorrow, then," Ariel said, interrupting my memory. She pivoted on one foot and hurried after Melissa.

Kaylee stopped, her shoulders hunching, when she saw Melissa and Ariel walking away. Before I could reach her, she spun around and ran, knocking against people who crowded the sidewalk.

"Kaylee!" I raced after her.

From the way everyone was turning and looking at her, I knew she was crying. When she saw me following her, she dodged into the crosswalk as a black Lexus whipped around a taxi. Kaylee froze as the woman driver slammed on her brakes. "Don't you know you're supposed to look before you step into the street?" the driver yelled.

"My light was green!" Kaylee slammed her fist on the car hood. "Do you think it's my fault you almost killed me?"

The driver rolled up her window as Kaylee rounded the car and seized the driver's door handle. *Clack!* All four doors locked.

"It's easy to break into a car," Kaylee threatened. "If I wanted your bucket, I'd just jack it."

My heart skittered. People were watching. A few had lifted their phones to take pictures.

Kaylee blew out a breath and then, steeling herself, eased her sweater sleeves over her fists and continued across the street.

I didn't chase after her this time. She was acting too erratic, and I was afraid she'd do something so completely reckless that we'd both end up in jail.

I missed my friend, the real Kaylee, and wondered if she was struggling, trying to find her way back to the person she had once been. I knew what had changed her, or at least, I thought I did. She had been with a guy, a secret she'd told only me. She'd believed she'd found that forever kind of love, but the guy had merely wanted a toy. She never told me who he was, only that she still wrote his name on the soles of her shoes so she could grind him into the dirt every day.

Friday morning, after Omar frisked me, he sat back on the couch where he'd been cleaning guns. The door to the closet under the stairs was open, revealing a stockpile of weapons. He dropped the mag from his Beretta and slid a bore snake into the barrel while I continued to the back porch.

The moment I stepped into the kitchen, the smell of urine hit me. The puppies had toppled their box and escaped the back porch. Their puddles spotted the linoleum. I found them flat on the floor, their snouts jammed into the narrow opening behind a floorboard that they had pried loose from the wall.

"You're too small to hunt rats," I scolded, pulling them away.

They nipped at my fingers and dashed back to the hole without even wagging their tails to greet me. I righted their box, braced it in a corner with a chair, then caught the puppies and set them inside where they whined until I fed them.

After wiping up their puddles, I knelt beside the dislodged floorboard. Nails, hammered into the backside, held tightly stretched strings that led over a trail of mouse droppings into the dark. Curious, I leaned down, the musky odor of mice breezing over me, and saw more strings leading to a gap between the floor and the outside wall. Maybe Dante had tied mousetraps to the ends.

Sitting up, I pinched the first string and reeled in whatever had been caught. A triple-wrapped plastic bag sealed with duct tape slid out of the crevice onto the floor in front of me, yellowish white rocks inside. Blood drained from my head, leaving me lightheaded with fear. I had found Trek's stash. People were killed for knowing less.

My fingers shaking, I shoved the bag back into its hiding place, then pressed the floorboard against the wall. It curved out again, buckling as if water had warped the wood. I was certain it hadn't stuck out so far before.

A sound broke through my panic. I thought I heard the wind chimes. My body tensed, cold sweat pricking my face, as I listened. Glass clinked against shells that jangled loudly. Someone was coming down the stairs.

Using all my strength, I tried to work the floorboard into place, my heart hammering so loudly I almost missed the tread of footsteps in the dining room. I sprang to my feet, the floorboard still bulging away from the wall, and turned as Satch and Rico entered the kitchen, their voices hushed.

Rico glanced up, his sudden alarm reflecting the anxiety he saw on my face. "What's wrong?"

"You startled me," I said with a forced laugh. Then to turn

their attention away from my nervousness, I quickly added, "Did I tell you that my jump-in is Saturday?"

Satch surveyed the room, his eyes glancing at the counter, the cupboards and ceiling, looking for anything that might have upset me, before he said, "You told us."

"Of course I did." I laughed again, too loudly, praying they didn't look down at the floor behind my feet. The drugs belonged to Trek, not to Core 9. Satch would understand the deadly consequences of stealing from Trek. But Rico wouldn't care. He'd take the drugs and, if he did, Trek would never stop until he caught him.

"Don't worry about the jump-in." Rico touched my cheek, his hand warm against my clammy skin. "You're going to make us proud."

When he stepped back, his gaze swept over the floor behind me. I watched him closely, but his smile never faltered. Maybe he hadn't seen the jutting floorboard.

"We got business to take care of," Satch reminded Rico, who nodded and followed him outside.

When the door closed, I fell against the wall and slid down to the floor. Still shaking, I worked the floorboard into place. It was like a puzzle, with slots and niches into which the board had to slide.

Feeling better now that I had narrowly avoided a catastrophe, I raced outside and caught up to Satch and Rico, their strides outpacing my jog as we hurried on to school. Their silence worried me until I saw the twitch in Rico's face. Trek had sent them on a mission.

Unexpectedly, they stopped in the dead-end street next to the school, where the drill team was practicing. Thirty-nine girls dressed in electric-blue jumpsuits and one boy lifted their arms in unison, the blue ribbons attached to their wands swirling over their heads as they kicked high, their smiles exaggerated in a show of teeth.

After a moment, I realized that Satch and Rico weren't watching the practice as I had thought. They were studying the still-wet graffiti painted on the street that read like a newspaper. The green color told me Danny was slinging. The arrow pointed toward the Borderlands, where buyers could find him. The numbers, standing for letters in the alphabet, were a menu of the drugs he was offering. Today he had sprayed a *3*, for crack, and a *16*, for *paco*, cocaine paste.

At the end of the street, near the roadblock, Danny stepped out from behind a hedge of weeds that teemed with gnats. His audacity stunned me. He was openly selling to users who normally bought from Trek, while flirting with someone who remained hidden from my view.

Stealthily, Satch crept alongside the drill team, ducking under the ribbons that looped in front of him, Rico close behind him. When they broke into a run, the sudden noise made Danny look up. He saw Satch and Rico lunging toward him and smiled; then, flashing his gang sign, he whistled shrilly to alert his homeboys and launched himself into a run.

Danny smashed through a thicket of spindly trees, startling dozens of sparrows into flight. Satch and Rico charged into the flock of frightened birds and disappeared into the Borderlands after him.

I started to turn away when Ariel came out from behind the weeds, huge sunglasses covering her eyes. She eased around the students who had been waiting to buy from Danny, her hair shimmering in the sunlight.

The drill team started practicing again, their ribbons creating a tangle of shadows that flickered over me as I hurried toward Ariel.

"Why were you talking to Danny?" I asked when I met up with her.

"He wanted me to buy," she said indifferently.

I knew she was lying. "Danny would never try to sell to you. Everyone knows you don't do drugs."

"He did." She lifted her sunglasses and set them on her head, her eyes sad, despairing even. She'd been crying.

"What's wrong?" I asked, her conversation with Danny suddenly unimportant.

"Someone broke into our garage last night and stole all the tools my dad needs for his work."

"Will insurance cover it?" I asked. Her dad worked as a handyman and sometimes got bigger jobs painting houses.

"Who's got money for insurance?" she said, watching the drill team. "The theft just made me realize that even if I make it through high school without getting killed, I'm never going to California. I'm stuck here."

"That's not true."

"Look at how hard my parents work, and they keep sliding backward. There's no escape from this place."

"You're creative. You'll do it."

She snorted softly. "I'm tired of teachers talking us up with stories about the American dream. Every year, they show us the same faded photographs of people who've made it out of neighborhoods like ours. Do teachers do that in middle-class schools?"

I shrugged. "How would I know?"

"They don't," Ariel said with certainty. "They don't have to, because those kids know the world is open to them. But for us, escape is a lie. It's like we live behind the Berlin Wall. We can see the West, we can even visit, we just can't live there."

On a field trip to the Newseum, Ariel and I had stared up at the huge block of concrete, part of the original wall that the Soviets had built to stop the flow of East Germans into West Berlin. We had understood that the wall surrounding us, though invisible, was just as formidable.

"I'll only get out of here if I'm sent to prison in another state," Ariel said.

"Go home," I ordered. "You shouldn't be at school when you're like this. You'll get into a fight, or worse."

"What's the matter?" Melissa asked as she joined us.

"The same old thing," Ariel said. "We're trapped."

"Stop thinking about the world outside," I said, nudging Ariel. "Just concentrate on how good you're going to feel Monday when we come back to school. Right, Melissa?"

"I decided not to do the jump-in," Melissa said softly.

"You've been talking about this since eighth grade," I said. "What happened?"

"Trek thinks I should do the *rollins* instead," Melissa said, looking away.

"Are you stupid?" Ariel punched Melissa's arm, hard enough

to make her cry out, then added, "No guy wants his girlfriend to pull a train."

I tried to ban the mental images that were gathering in my mind. Instead of being beaten into the gang, Melissa was going to roll a pair of dice, and whatever number came up would decide how many guys she'd have sex with in order to join Core 9.

"Trek says it's the only choice for a girl who's as beautiful as I am." Melissa brushed back her hair. "He's worried I'll get hurt. You've seen the scars on Twyla's face. Her nose is still crooked."

"You can't let Trek decide. You've only been seeing him for two weeks," I said. "What's he done to you?"

"He makes me happy," Melissa replied.

"If you're sexed into the gang," Ariel argued, "no one will respect you. Even guys like Dante will think they can own you." She pointed to the school entrance where Dante stood, trying to look tough with a cigarette tucked behind his ear and an AK-47 pendant swinging from a chain around his neck.

"Dante won't bother me," Melissa countered. "No one will with Trek standing by my side."

"Do you think he's going to be there forever?" I asked.

Melissa gave me a stony smile. "Do you think I'm going to live forever? I got a year maybe, and I'm going to live it the best I can." She swirled around, the scent of her new musky perfume spinning into the air, and walked away from us.

"Trek's got Melissa hypnotized with all that money he's spending on her," Ariel said. "She never would have decided this on her own."

"We're going to stop her," I said grimly.

"How?"

"We'll take the dice from her and beat her into the gang ourselves."

"Can we do that?" Ariel asked.

"Of course we can," I said. "We're outlaws. We can do anything we want."

8

The night of the jump-in, Ariel and I crossed the park, the air cool and flecked with ash from the fires burning inside metal trash cans that formed a large circle under the trees. Sparks crackled off the flames and twisted into the wind, smoke swirling around the 3Ts and seven other homegirls who waited for us in the center.

I thought Ariel was watching the red embers spiral into the leaves, until I glimpsed a man-size silhouette crouched on a branch. The wind shifted, bending the leaves, and the flickering light revealed a young man, dressed in black, who pulled himself onto a higher branch out of view.

"Who'd want to watch us get beat up?" I asked, trying to find his outline again.

"Some wannabe probably," Ariel replied, smearing Vaseline over her face so the punches would glide off her skin.

"No wannabe would have the guts to show up here," I said.

"A homeless person, then," Ariel snapped. "Who cares?"

I stared at her, suddenly understanding. "What's going on?" I asked.

"Just forget about it, all right? I want to get this over with."

I didn't say more because we had stopped in front of the fire near the picnic tables, where Rico and Satch stood with their homeboys, drinking beer, apparently unaware of the intruder in the tree. The Core 9 girls would beat us into the gang, but the homeboys could watch. More homies were wandering up the street from the party at Trek's house, the music from inside echoing into the night.

My nervous fingers worked my hair into a braid that I tucked into the back of my long-sleeved T-shirt. I'd worn tight-fitting old jeans that I could trash if they got too bloody and torn, but my real preparation for the jump-in had started years ago, when I'd practiced dodging punches and deflecting blows because I had to learn how to fight to survive in the neighborhood.

Dante glanced at me, then laughed and said something to Omar, probably making fun of how scared Ariel and I appeared. The prickling in my stomach had surprised me. I hadn't expected to feel so afraid.

Omar remained stone-faced, ignoring Dante, who continued to laugh until Rico slammed his hands into Dante's shoulders and gave him an edgy stare. The laughter stopped so completely I could hear the flames crackling.

"We're cool," Dante said, backing away from the confrontation, his palms up in a gesture of surrender.

Rico waited until Dante left the park before he made his way to me. I handed him my cell phone to hold, then took out my earrings, which had been a gift from my dad, and gave them to him as well.

He slipped everything into his pocket. "Stay relaxed," he instructed.

"Hey, Toughness." Satch joined us and handed me a fistful of cotton. "I brought this so you could protect your smile."

"Thanks," I said with a nervous laugh before pushing wads of cotton between my lips and teeth.

Hugging me, Rico whispered, "Show them what you got."

Tara signaled for me to go first. My heart, already racing on adrenaline, knocked against my ribs. I kicked off my shoes. Barefoot, I was more agile, able to jump, pivot, and spin, skills I needed because I wasn't allowed to fight back, only protect myself.

"See you soon," I said. The beating would last for sixty seconds.

When I stepped into the circle, Tanya flung her arms around me. "Welcome, Blaise."

Her friendliness put me on guard. I bent my knees, my toes squeezing the grass. The moment Tara began the count, Tanya tried to throw me to the ground. I kept my balance and broke away, only to crash into punches that battered my shoulders and head, each blow sending a shock through my body.

I bounced back, dipped, and spun, avoiding several hits until more girls jostled around me, closing in tight. So many fists came at me that when I ducked away from one I bobbed up into another. Panic snaked into my stomach. I had been arrogant to think I could escape the beating with dips and spins.

"... sixteen ... seventeen ... eighteen ..."

Something razor-edged sliced my scalp, a ring or maybe an acrylic nail. Blood trickled through my hair, dripping warm onto my forehead. I blinked and the color red seeped into my vision. In the second that I paused to wipe my eyes, Tanya caught me and socked my arm, her strength staggering.

". . . twenty-five . . . twenty-six . . . twenty-seven . . ."

I stood motionless, recovering. The dagger-sharp pain renewed its bite with each breath, while all around me girls continued to punch my neck and chest, their jabs nothing compared with what Tanya could do.

Through the crimson haze that blurred my vision, I saw Tanya coming at me again. My heart skipping beats, I stumbled backward, eluding her, until four other girls penned me in, their fists battering my head.

Panting, I worked hard to deflect their blows, my arms catching their strikes, new bruises throbbing under tender skin. Unable to bear more, I spun to escape them, nearly tripping over their legs, and rammed into Tanya, who swung her hand into my stomach.

". . . forty-two . . . forty-three . . . forty-four . . ."

Air left my lungs in a *whoosh*. My abdomen cramped with an explosion of pain as spasms squeezed my chest. I couldn't breathe. I needed air. Faces and fires rotated around me, melding together in a spin. I steadied myself, fighting the dizziness. If I fell to the ground, the beating would be worse.

". . . fifty . . . fifty-one . . . fifty-two . . ."

Under a barrage of fists, I stumbled, trying to avoid Tanya, who swung again and struck my nose. New pain seared through my head and crackled down my spine. I wanted to give up, yell for them to stop—but if I did, I'd lose my chance to become part of Core 9 and end up a nobody.

I stepped back, sucking at air through my swelling nostrils, only to gag on the blood that gurgled in the back of my throat. My fear spiked. I could not survive another hit from Tanya, who seemed to materialize in front of me. Her knuckles landed on my cheek, near my right eye. Tiny light-comets streaked through my vision. My knees gave way and, as I started to fall, I thought of my grandmother, how my death would destroy her.

". . . fifty-eight . . . fifty-nine . . . sixty!"

"Stop!" Tara yelled, jumping in front of me. She braced me against her, holding me up, and took the last hits on her own back.

Slowly, my strength returned. I balanced precariously on quaking legs and faced Tara, who used my blood to write *Core 9* across my face, each letter stinging my raw skin.

When she finished, Tanya began to jump from one foot to the other, back and forth, faster and faster, pounding the ground in praise of me. The other girls joined in and stomped with her until the earth hollered with a stampede of feet. Joy raced through me. I had done it. My heart soared with pride.

A calm I hadn't felt for a long time spread through me. No matter what happened now, I would always have a family.

The homegirls—my homegirls—took turns hugging me, and when each one pulled back, she had my blood on her face, which no one wiped away, another tribute to me.

Taking deep gulping breaths, I limped back to Ariel, who waited outside the circle, her arms open. As I started to hug her, other arms encircled me, turning me around. With only the use of my left eye, my right swollen shut, I stared up at Satch, who looked at me intensely.

"Are you okay?" His fingers brushed through my snarled hair, the undone braid, and over the cut on my scalp, and when his palms came back wet with my blood, he cradled me against his hard body before he gave me to Rico, who wrapped his arms around me.

"I'm okay," I muttered, barely able to open my mouth and take out the blood-soaked cotton.

Leaning against Rico, I stared at the red imprint of my face on Satch's white T-shirt and thought about the way he had held me. I had sensed that he'd wanted to say something more, but my head was too muddled with pain and dizziness to know for sure.

"My turn," Ariel said, pulling me from my thoughts. "Wish me good luck."

"Watch out for Tanya," I tried to whisper, my lips sticking together, gluey with blood.

"I'll be careful." She slid between the fires, her boldness not fooling me. She was scared. Probably more than I had been, since she'd witnessed what they'd done to me.

The wind quickened as she walked into the circle. The trees, bending with the gusts, plunged their branches into the fires and swung back with leaves aflame. A halo of blazes crackled overhead, the firelight writhing over the homegirls, who eased in closer, surrounding Ariel.

Tara began the count and the homegirls attacked. Fists

hammered Ariel, who bobbed, then stooped and swerved as the wind swept more branches through the fires. Tiny flames climbed over a new tapestry of leaves.

Ariel glanced up while trying to fend off the blows, searching for the person in the tree, and not watching Tanya.

When I started to cry out and warn her, Rico shushed me. "She's got to do it on her own."

Tanya plowed into Ariel. The impact threw her to the ground. She landed on her stomach. Her head bobbed up and she seemed confused to find herself sprawled in the grass. Before she could stand, Twyla kicked her forehead and the skin split open. Ariel tucked her head down and, guarding her face with her arms, disappeared in the tangle of kicking feet as the homegirls encircled her.

I looked away and became aware of Satch, standing alone, behind his friends, his stillness giving me the impression that he had been watching me for a while. He smiled, then grabbed a six-pack off the picnic table and walked away.

I might have gone after him but Rico grasped my shoulders, his touch trying to fortify me for what I was going to see.

"It's over," he said. "At least Ariel's standing."

The wind had toppled three trashcans and scattered the burning debris. Black smoke, speckled with glowing embers, stirred around the homegirls. Twyla and Tanya held Ariel between them, while Tara wrote *Core 9* in the blood that covered her face.

After the homegirls had finished embracing her, she hobbled toward me, glancing furtively up into the trees before she fell into my arms, her cheek slick with blood. "We did it," I rasped, my fingers gliding over the knots that covered her back and arms, and probably resembled the blackened bumps on her hand and chin.

"Help me walk," she said jaggedly, her voice not as garbled as mine. "I don't want to have to be carried."

I nodded and, with Ariel leaning against my throbbing body, the older girls paraded us down the street, past the homeboys who sat on Trek's porch, drinking forties and holding guns. A few pulled out their cell phones and took pictures of us before we entered the crowded living room, where music vibrated the floor, the air hot and filled with layers of smoke that smelled of cigarettes, skunk, and burnt plastic.

Though we were supposed to continue on to the kitchen to celebrate, I leaned Ariel against a wall and surveyed the crowd. Trek sat on the couch, his arm around Melissa, who wore a clingy yellow dress. Her silver bracelets glimmered, reflecting light from a line of candles on the window ledge. She was already shaking the dice, her fingernails manicured, bright pink.

Clumsily, my back and neck stiff, my head aching, I shoved my way through the guys gathered around her, snatched the dice before anyone could count the dots, and fell flat on the table. Pain ruptured in my side as I struggled to my feet and lunged at Melissa, my blood splattering the homeboys, who laughed at my slow-motion boxing when I tried to beat her.

"What are you doing?" Melissa slapped my hands away.

Trek nodded to Omar, who wrested the dice from me and gave them back to Melissa.

"Change your mind." My swollen lips slurred my words, my teeth aching as I spoke. "Go in the circle. It's not too late."

"And end up like you?" Melissa said, wiping my blood from her cheek. "I'm the one who made the right choice. You're going to be scarred for life." Then, acting coquettish, she looked at the homeboys and rolled the dice across the smear of blood that I had left on the table.

When I tried to lunge forward again, Omar blocked my way and I stumbled against him. "Come on, Blaise," he said. "I'll have to stop you if you try, and I don't want to hurt you."

Conceding defeat, I rested my forehead against his chest, too weak to fight. He cupped my elbows, seeming to sense how close I was to collapsing.

"Nine," the homeboys roared.

My stomach pitched. I turned away, knowing I could not possibly feel worse and, in the same breath, I did. Ariel was slipping down the wall, blood pouring from the cut on her forehead. I struggled back to her, barely able to make my way around the couples who had started dancing now that the homegirls had returned from the jump-in.

"Did you beat Melissa into the gang?" Ariel asked, her teeth chattering.

I held her against me, her skin too cold, and tried to warm her with my body. Fear shot through me when I placed my fingers on her pulse and felt a strange threading of beats that rushed together.

"We need to get you to a doctor," I muttered.

"I think it's too late." Ariel's eyelids fluttered and she slid through my arms, her weight too much for me to hold.

I glanced back at Melissa, hoping she would see Ariel and help me, but Melissa was already heading up the stairs with a pack of homeboys.

I trotted alongside Satch and Rico, who carried Ariel between them, her head lolling against Rico's arm. The cut on her forehead still bled, her blood dripping onto the sidewalk. We were taking her to Irwin, an old man who had been a medic in Vietnam. Though I supposed his medical practice was illegal, no one snitched, because we needed him to treat injuries that the police might want to investigate.

We took the shortcut through the park. Fires sputtered in the trees and spilled fiery leaves that whirled around us. The heat grew intense near the picnic tables, the singed grass hot beneath my feet. I had hoped to grab my forgotten shoes, but they smoldered where I had left them, scorched and ruined.

When I dodged a burning branch that swept in front of me, I glimpsed someone creeping through the billowing smoke.

Rico slowed his pace. "Someone's trailing us."

"There's no time for a confrontation," I pleaded, my words slurring together.

"Go," Satch said as fire engines rumbled to a stop on the

opposite side of the park. The revolving lights on the trucks flashed over the swirling soot while firefighters connected hoses to the hydrant.

Two blocks later, we arrived at Irwin's house. Boards were missing from the sunken porch, as were the stairs. A single cinder block functioned as a step.

I trusted Irwin, but the blood oozing from Ariel's forehead worried me. *How much blood could a person lose and still live?* "Maybe we should take Ariel to the hospital where they can give her a transfusion."

"How are you going to explain the way you look to the cops who'll be on duty in the emergency room?" Rico asked.

"Car accident," I said.

"Cops will swarm all over you," Satch argued, "because the two of you look beaten."

The door scraped open and Irwin stepped onto his sagging porch, a red robe tied over his pajamas. "Bring Ariel inside. I'll decide if she needs to go to the hospital."

I followed Satch and Rico across the dark living room and into the kitchen. A fluorescent light buzzed overhead and reflected off Irwin's old-fashioned aviator glasses. He stretched latex gloves over his hands before he sat on a stool, his knees sliding under a cot covered with a white sheet that smelled of bleach.

Satch and Rico set Ariel down while Irwin broke a plastic stick. The scent of ammonia bore into my sinuses.

"Smelling salts," Irwin explained, waving the stick under Ariel's nose.

Her chest rose in a sharp breath that she coughed out in a blood-tinged spray. Groggily, she glanced around, and when her gaze settled on me, she smiled. "Blaise, you look like raw meat."

"I can't look as bad as you do," I said, keeping the mood light, though I wanted to fall on my knees and offer a prayer of gratitude that Ariel wasn't dead.

"You both look like road kill," Irwin said without any humor in his voice. He swabbed something orange over Ariel's forehead, then covered the split skin with gauze and pressed his hand over it. The bleeding stopped.

"My anesthetics were stolen, so I don't have anything to give you for the pain," Irwin apologized.

I glanced at the medicine cabinet where he had pointed and a face startled me. I almost screamed before I realized I was looking at my own reflection. My right eye, swollen shut, bulged out in an ugly knob. A sludgy mess of lumps and clots covered my forehead and cheeks. Blood had dried on my neck, caking in hard scabs. I looked like something that had crawled out of a grave.

"Maybe I'll need to give you a few stitches, too, Blaise," Irwin said before he scrutinized Satch and Rico, who crowded the kitchen, ash and bits of blackened leaves flaking off their clothes, their sooty tracks a mess across the floor.

"You two go on," Irwin said. "Blaise and Ariel are going to spend the night here so I can keep an eye on them, but there's no reason for you to stay."

Rico and Satch lingered anyway, looking worried.

"Are you waiting for a kiss good-bye?" I teased Rico, to let him know I'd be okay.

To my surprise, he gently placed his lips on mine. "Congratulations, Blaise," he whispered after he pulled away. "You're now one of the elite." He pressed my cell phone into my hands along with my earrings.

"We'll check on you tomorrow," Satch said as Rico nudged him toward the door.

After they left, Irwin opened a small packet that read *surgical suture* across the front and pulled out a curved, eyeless needle with an attached length of thread. "Ariel, I'm going to have to rely on your grit to keep you steady while I sew you up."

"All right." Her bruised fingers clenched the sides of the cot.

As I stepped closer to Ariel, a scrape at the back door distracted me. The doorknob jiggled slightly. Someone was working the lock. I glanced at Irwin, who hadn't noticed the sound. He was busy swabbing alcohol across Ariel's forehead.

"Blaise," Irwin said, looking up at me. "This might be hard for you to watch. Why don't you wait on the front porch? I'll get you when I've finished with Ariel."

"He's afraid my screaming will make you run," Ariel joked bravely.

"That's a definite possibility," Irwin said grimly.

I nodded, but the sound at the back door had made me suspicious—not of Irwin, of course, but of the person who had been following us in the park. I walked through the living room, opened the door, and clomped out on the porch, pretending to leave, then soundlessly eased back inside. I let the door close and waited.

Soon after, I heard the back door open.

"You can't barge in here," Irwin protested, sounding annoyed but not alarmed.

"I need to see Ariel," a voice replied.

"Danny," Ariel whispered with too much happiness.

I listened to Danny murmur sweet things to Ariel. Though my heart longed to hear such words spoken to me, I pushed aside any romantic fantasy and settled on my apprehension. Ariel was going to get herself killed.

10

As the sun was rising, I walked Ariel home. Her mother screamed when she saw us, her shrieks a mix of horror and anger and, finally, relief. She locked Ariel into her arms and, as Ariel's dried blood rubbed off on the white uniform that her mother wore to the beauty shop, a memory leaked into my thoughts. In my mind, I was four years old again, lying on the backseat of my father's car, unable to swallow the blood pouring into my throat fast enough to breathe.

The day had started out happy, with chocolate ice cream and coconut macaroons for breakfast while my mother laughed with one of the men who came around while my father worked. They had left me alone, which she frequently did and, by lunchtime, she had returned wearing a new white blouse that he had bought for her.

Later, when I had awakened from my nap, she was setting up the ironing board. I had scanned her face for warning signs, because sometimes the men who visited her left her with a craving for a different life.

As she'd picked up the iron, her expression had become too still, her cold stare alerting me that I should hide, but then she'd said, *You're in my way, Blaise.*

The sweetness in her tone had confused me. I'd smiled as the iron swung into my face.

By the time I had drifted back into consciousness, my father had come home from work. I heard him yell, *Are you trying to kill her?*

It was an accident! My mother had screamed. *Blaise is always in the way.*

My mother had refused to hold me while my father drove us to the hospital. She hadn't wanted to get blood on her new white blouse. My father had heard my struggle and stopped the car, picked me off the backseat, and forced me into my mother's unwilling arms, which remained stiff, even after he'd told her that I would drown in my own blood if she didn't hold me upright.

After the surgery, two police officers had questioned me. I told them that I had gotten in my mother's way and was sorry for ruining her blouse.

With that memory drifting behind me, I sloshed through the wet ash that covered the park and tried to call Melissa again. She still didn't answer and I left another message. Though I needed to find her, I had to see my grandmother first.

I slammed through the front door. "I'm home!"

"I was just going out to look for you!" my grandmother shouted from the kitchen. "Where have you been?"

She charged into the living room. Her anger flared and vanished, the car keys tumbling from her hand when she saw my bloodied face. Her mouth fell open as she took in air, and then she screamed.

"Lord have mercy, what happened to you?" She petted my face, soothing my skin with her cool palms before she pulled me into her arms, my dried blood soiling her clothes.

I exhaled, relaxing, and repeated the lie I had practiced on Ariel's mother. "Ariel and I had an accident on Dante's motor scooter. We spent the night at Irwin's house so he could watch Ariel, who was hurt worse than I was."

"I thought I told you to stay off that contraption." My grandmother didn't question my lie, because she wanted to believe that I was a good girl who thought daring was a ride on a rickety scooter. "You can't take such risks. Promise me you'll be more careful!"

"I promise," I said, breathing in the traces of Pine-Sol that clung to her. She had once worn a sweet honeysuckle fragrance, a luxury she had given up for her dream of seeing me in college. "Life is going to get better for you, Grandma," I whispered. "You'll see."

"What I want to *see* is you cleaned up and in bed." She held my face, her smile gentle, forgiving me for my stupidity. "I'll call the school tomorrow and tell them you'll be out for a couple of days."

In the bathroom, I sat on the edge of the tub, my muscles too tender to peel off my clothes. I took the scissors that my grandmother used to trim her hair and cut off my T-shirt, jeans, and underwear. I had hoped a shower would ease my pain, but when I stepped under the spray, the water stung like nettles. My raw skin couldn't bear the heat that my knotted muscles craved. I dried off and spread the ointment that Irwin had given me over my face and the tiny stitches on my scalp.

Exhausted, I needed to sleep but, after pulling on my sweats, I dragged myself downstairs, back to the kitchen, and found my grandmother sitting at the table, her Bible open to 1 Corinthians.

I touched her arm, startling her. "You don't have to stay up and take care of me. Go on to bed."

She stood, then drew me to her and kissed my forehead. "You better eat something," she said wearily, leaving the room. "And get some rest."

I choked on the little bit of cereal that I tried to swallow and then washed out my mouth with salt water as Irwin had instructed. My lips stung, but my tongue felt better, no longer gluey.

The moment I heard my grandmother's fan, I grabbed my purse and left.

A short walk later, my head throbbing, I steadied myself against the shaking in my legs and knocked on Melissa's door. When no one answered, I stole the key from a tin box hidden under the steps and let myself inside.

A scattering of cockroaches fled in front of me as I passed a closed door that most likely led into a pantry. I set the key on the kitchen counter, the quiet unnerving until the refrigerator cycled on in a loud hum that rose and fell in an annoying rhythm.

Though I had often watched Melissa take the key from its hiding place, she had never invited me inside. Seeing the emptiness in which she lived filled me with sorrow. There wasn't a table or even a chair in the kitchen. The only color besides the graying yellow of the walls and linoleum came from the velvet seams of black mold that lined the windowsill and tiles behind the sink.

For a moment, I wondered if I could have broken into the wrong apartment. I saw nothing of my vibrant friend who, as early as seventh grade, had dazzled the boys with her flamboyant style, wearing pink and purple ribbons around her wrists to draw attention to herself. She had painted a star beside her eye, sometimes silver, sometimes blue, a beauty mark to let everyone know she was destined to become a celebrity.

I crept into the living room where Melissa's mother, a day sleeper like my grandmother, slept on the couch, orange foam plugs in her ears. I did a complete turn, but the only door I saw opened to a bathroom. Maybe Melissa didn't have a bedroom and, like Rico, slept on the floor. If so, then she hadn't come home last night.

My stomach churned. I started to leave when I passed the pantry door again. This time, I turned the knob and stepped into the long, windowless room.

A nightlight glowed in the socket, the light falling over Melissa, who lay curled on a thick gray blanket, the kind given to the homeless in winter. Her hands pressed against her abdomen, the yellow dress she had worn earlier barely covering her now.

"I tried to call you," I whispered, not sure if she was awake.

"I lost my phone last night," she said dully.

She lifted her head, her eyes flat. A chill passed through me. I sensed no life behind her gaze. Without looking at her, I sat on the edge of the blanket. I didn't want her to see my tears. She seemed more beaten than Ariel.

"I was worried about you," I said, trying not to breathe the awful smell that came off her, of fear and sweat, and something worse.

Her misery crowded the silence between us. I touched her back and felt her flinch, her shoulders and back stiffening. I pulled my hand away and waited.

After a long moment, she whispered, "They watched."

Revulsion shot through me. *Dear God, please, no.* I didn't want to hear.

"All of them," she rasped. "They stood in a circle waiting their turn and watched." Her vacant gaze left me and focused on the wall. "It wasn't anything like I'd imagined . . . it wasn't like loving someone."

I wondered if Trek had told her that it would be.

Her face squinched and she drew her knees up to her chest. When her body relaxed, she said, "Some of them came at me twice. They must have, because—"

"Can I get you something?" I interrupted, suddenly a coward who wanted an excuse to leave the room, grab four aspirin, and escape into sleep.

Melissa said nothing, but when I looked into her deadened eyes, I sensed her accusation and disappointment. She needed me. I couldn't fail her like I had last night.

"Go on." I sat stock-still, powerless to hold back my tears, as Melissa continued.

"Trek never came into the room," she said, her eyes focused on the wall again. "I kept thinking he'd stop them."

Anger seethed inside me. I hated Trek for not protecting her.

I hated myself even more for abandoning her. I should have gone back with a gun.

"But I wouldn't have wanted Trek to see me like that," Melissa said, already making excuses for him. "Omar helped me dress. Then he carried me home because I couldn't walk."

"And now?" I asked, feeling the weight of my heart. "How are you now?"

"I can't even pee, but that doesn't matter, because I hurt too much to get up and walk to the bathroom. I told my mom I had cramps and was staying home from school tomorrow."

"We should go see Irwin," I said.

"I don't want him to know what I've done." She tried to hold back a sob. "I'm so worthless."

"You're not worthless." I stretched out beside her.

"I feel the difference," she whispered, letting me pull her into my arms. "I've lost what I was. I'm nothing now."

"Don't say that. It's not your fault. You did what you had to do to survive. That's all it is. Survival. Nothing more."

"Maybe," she said, her tears warm on my neck. "But I have this feeling . . ."

"What?"

". . . like the gates of hell have opened for me."

11

Melissa whimpered in her sleep, her hair wet and sticking to her face. I touched her shoulder, the skin feverishly hot and slippery with sweat. Her leg twitched as if she were trying to run from me. I drew my fingers back and pulled myself up. My muscles had locked and the simple movement of standing sent painful spasms through my body.

In the kitchen, I ran water and sipped it from my cupped hands. Since the jump-in, I'd eaten nothing, and my stomach gurgled around the liquid, which tasted of mold and old pipes. I stopped drinking when nausea became stronger than my thirst.

I filled a glass for Melissa and set it on the floor within her reach, next to the packet of antibiotics that I'd gotten for her from Irwin. She didn't need to take another pill for two hours. Even so, I hated leaving her, but I was worried about my grandmother and needed to get home before she found my unmade bed. She might think I'd wandered off, delirious, and I didn't want her calling the cops.

I stepped outside, the air suddenly fresh, and took in huge gasping breaths. After locking the door and hiding the key, I started forward, my body trembling from hunger.

Near my home, a sixth sense drew my attention to an old Chevy rolling down the street. Four girls inside wore a masquerade of sunglasses and pink baseball caps. I shuffled backward until I stood in dappled shadows, next to a rattling swamp cooler that dripped water. My feet sank into the mud as the car eased to the curb in front of my grandmother's roses.

Gatita got out, her silver rings flashing in the sunlight, and left something on my porch. Though I couldn't see it well from this distance, I guessed it was a toy wolf, like those sold at the zoo, to let me know the Lobos knew where I lived.

As soon as the car sped away, I plunged out of the shadows in a breakneck dash toward my house. I only had seconds before the car might return. I clasped the handrail and pulled myself up to the porch, jammed my key into the lock, then stumbled inside, pain raging in my head. I closed the door and fell against it, resting there until the darkness pulsing in my vision slowed; then I started for the stairs.

The run across the street had strained my back and, when I lifted my foot, cramps twisted up my spine. I pitched forward and fell hard, forced to wait until the dizziness and nausea eased before I crawled up to the landing, where I clutched the newel post and pulled myself to my feet. I staggered to my room and passed out across my bed.

When I opened my eyes again, my grandmother was kneeling

beside me, dressed for work. Her breath, flowing over me, smelled faintly like nail polish remover. The scent told me she hadn't eaten. I listened to her prayer and wasn't even aware of falling back asleep until a dank breeze roused me from my slumber, cold across my face.

I was shivering but in too much pain to get up and close the window. I started to pull the covers over me when a bolt of awareness shot through me. The pink curtains weren't billowing; even the ruffles lay in motionless curls.

The draft had to be coming from the attic. Someone had used the passageway to break into my home. Anyone who lived in the row houses on this block could have crept through the old escape route. One home was vacant, a foreclosure. Police had driven out squatters months before. Maybe new ones had settled in, discovered the holes and—*Gatita!* Had she found her way inside?

Fully awake, I slipped my hand over the covers until I touched the hammer. I forced my stiff fingers to clasp the handle as the floorboards creaked beneath a prowler's weight. My nerves hummed, ready to launch my battered body into an attack.

When a silhouette slid over the wall beside my bed, I took one last breath, my body buzzing with adrenaline, and sat up, pain exploding inside me.

Satch spun around, a gun in his hand, his startled face lit from the streetlight. "What are you doing, Blaise? You about scared me to death."

"Why are you here?" I asked, setting the hammer aside. "Has someone been hurt?" My mind skidded from one catastrophe to the next. "Was Rico shot?"

"I'm right here." Rico held up the plastic wolf that had been on my stoop. "We didn't want you to be alone if Lobos decided to pay you another visit."

I smiled, falling back on my pillow, and let a memory carry me to the summer between sixth and seventh grades, when I'd met Rico.

My father had died and, though my own grief was weighing on me, I had tried to hide it from my grandmother. When I needed to cry, I would hide near the Borderlands beneath the branches of a fallen tree, so she wouldn't see my tears and feel worse.

Some days, Rico had watched me from the end of the alley near Tulley's while he drank a Coke. I had known he was a gangster, two years ahead of me in school, and Satch's best friend, but I had never spoken to him because his reputation had scared me.

One afternoon, when I had arrived at the tree, three homeless dopers were waiting for me. Before I could run, they had grabbed me. Rico had appeared from the shadows and, after beating them away, he'd sheltered me in his arms while I'd sobbed.

But I hadn't really become his friend until the first snow. I had been on my way to school, my teeth chattering, when he'd burst out of a yard.

He'd set a package the size of a shoebox on top of my books and had sprinted away, toward the Lobos' streets, the brittle ice splintering beneath his steps. The summer before, he had told me how he sometimes pretended to be a Lobo when he stole from Mass 5. I had sensed that he was doing that now to throw off whoever was chasing him.

I had continued walking toward school, amazed at my outward calm while inside my heart was racing. Seconds later, behind me, two Mass 5 gangsters had bolted out of the yard, pausing for a moment before following Rico's path in the shattered ice toward the Lobos' neighborhood.

That night, when I had opened the door, Rico had scanned the living room, as if he had expected to see a police officer waiting for him. I had a reputation, then, as a church girl.

Without a word, I gave him the package, still wrapped the way it had been when he'd set it on my books.

Grinning, he'd clenched his hand and waited until I had fisted mine, then he'd rapped my knuckles with his. "Till death do us part," he'd whispered.

I had finally become his friend.

12

Voices came from downstairs, the aroma of bacon and coffee drifting up with the laughter. I opened my eyes, sunlight stunning my vision, and tried to sit up, but pain kept me pinned to my bed.

Minutes later, a shadow passed over me, and then my grandmother's face hovered above mine, toast crumbs on her lips, a dot of grape jelly spotting her chin. Gently, she touched my bruised cheek. "Are you up to having visitors?"

When I nodded, I felt as if my brain was ripping away from my skull. The pain had gotten worse.

Tara, Tanya, and Twyla crowded into my room and stood in front of my window, their shadows flickering over my pink bedspread.

"Your friends brought food," my grandmother added. "Do you want me to scramble you some eggs?"

"Too sick to eat," I muttered, gratitude washing over me as I mouthed *thank you* to the 3Ts.

"I have to get some sleep," my grandmother said, excusing

herself. She kissed the top of my head, then left. Soon after, the hum from her bedroom fan began vibrating through my room.

"I brought stuff to make you feel better," Tara said, placing plastic bottles of chocolate syrup on my nightstand. "Your grandmother thinks it's medicine from Irwin, but it's my own concoction."

"Tara's a regular pharmacy," Tanya said as Twyla flopped down on the end of my bed, the mattress swaying when she criss-crossed her legs.

I forced my body up until I was leaning against the headboard.

Tanya caught my grimace. "Ariel's already sleeping through her pain. You would be, too, if you'd been home when we came by yesterday."

I ignored the question implied in her statement. I wasn't going to tell anyone about my visit with Melissa.

Tara squeezed chocolate syrup into a paper cup that she handed to me along with a white pill. From the size and roughness, I knew she'd made it herself. I set it on my tongue and could feel it dissolving, the granules cold and numbing my mouth. I swallowed the chocolate to wash it down and continued sipping to get rid of the bitter taste.

"You can't feed the dogs anymore," Tara said, taking the cup from me and placing it on my nightstand next to more pills. "That's no job for a gangster."

"I can't give them up," I said, sliding down to my pillow as the room began to tilt. My mind rose and fell on pleasurable waves that were carrying me away from the pain.

"Kaylee could feed them," Twyla sniggered.

"Trek would never let her into his house," Tanya said. "She'd poison the dogs and him, too."

"She's tough and crazy enough for Core 9," Tara said, rubbing alcohol over the skin between my index finger and thumb. "I wanted her."

"We all did," Tanya agreed.

When I tried to ask why they hadn't invited Kaylee to join Core 9, my deadened tongue refused to move. I needed to remember what the 3Ts had said, but already the drug was looping my thoughts with dreams. Their conversation fell away as darkness engulfed me.

Each time I awakened, I took another pill, until the afternoon when I came to without any pain. I knew I had been out for days, not hours. I had rolling memories of my grandmother feeding me and smearing antibiotics over my skin, her worried face near mine as she prayed. I remembered Satch coming into my room as well, but why would he spend his nights beside my bed when he could be hanging out with his homeboys? Still, I recalled him telling me stories about his wild adventures with Rico as I drifted in and out, but the more I thought about his visits, the more I became convinced that they were no more than drug-induced fantasies.

When I finally got out of bed, I felt jittery, but also amazingly good. I showered and, as I let the water take away my stiffness, I removed the bandage on the web between my index finger and thumb and stared at the *C9* that Tara had inked into my skin. I twisted my arm through the spray, admiring my tattoo from different angles.

As I dressed, my phone pinged. I opened a picture that Ariel had sent of the bright red gash on her forehead.

A second later, my call tone sounded and before I even said hello, Ariel spoke. "I'm worried about Melissa."

"You saw her?" I asked as I went downstairs to the kitchen.

"Yesterday. I had to go back to Irwin so he could check my stitches, and I stopped to see how she's doing."

"And?" I asked, opening a bag of potato chips that sat on the table.

"She seems so sad. I mean, I could feel it, like, her emotions were in the air. I had to ask her three times if she wanted something to eat, and finally I just went out and bought her a hamburger and fries."

"Did she eat them?"

"I'm not sure she even saw them. She just kept staring. I wanted to go back today, but something came up."

"I'll check on her," I said, already heading for the front door.

The streets were empty, the stillness so deep I could hear my bare feet slapping the sidewalk. I ducked under the tree branches near the back of the row house where Melissa lived and stopped when I heard Trek, who, I assumed, was talking to Melissa.

"It was your decision, so why are you feeling so sad?" he asked. "I only went along with what you wanted. Do you think I liked your choice? No guy wants his girl to do the *rollins*, but I stood by you. That's proof I love you, isn't it? So why are you taking it out on me?"

His words shocked me. I leaned against the moss-covered

bricks and pondered what I'd heard. Had Melissa become afraid of the jump-in and then blamed Trek for her decision to do the rollins? Maybe she had thought she'd be able to handle it the same way I had thought I'd be able to avoid a beating at my jump-in with dips and spins.

"Please, baby, talk to me," Trek pleaded. "What can I do to cheer you up? Just name it. I'll do anything."

I held my breath and peered around the corner. Trek and Melissa sat on the stoop. He had his arms around her, his head bent in front of her as if he were trying to get her to look at him instead of the ground. I had never seen Trek with his guard down before and I couldn't believe how vulnerable he seemed.

"I love you more than life itself," he said. "Please don't do this. Come back to me."

I waited until Trek had coaxed a smile from Melissa and then I walked home. Maybe he really did care about her.

13

Beyond the glare coming off the cars in the teachers' parking lot, the school security guards were trying to stop a fight between Lobos and Mass 5 gangsters that was escalating into a riot. I threaded my way around my classmates, who were watching the three-way brawl while more and more students pushed forward, straining to see.

A girl glanced at me and rammed her elbow into the side of her friend, her whisper soughing into the breeze. *Watch out. Move. Get out of her way.*

The chatter quieted as others became aware of me. Heads turned and the nudging began as I made my way through the crowd.

I was returning to school for the first time since the jump-in, wearing expensive tennis shoes that the 3Ts had bought for me. Though a few scratches still marred my face, the swelling had gone down and Irwin had removed my stitches. I had hemmed my skirt, nine inches above my knees, to flaunt that I was now Core 9. And a splotch of makeup covered the tattoo between my thumb and index finger, but everyone knew what I was concealing.

Suddenly, seeming to jump out of nowhere, Kaylee cut through the crowd and walked toward me, smiling. "Welcome back."

"Hey, Kaylee," I said, my face expressionless, though my mind was shouting, *Don't, Kaylee! Don't do anything stupid*.

"I heard you had the flu," she said, her jealousy filling the air between us.

"Is that what everyone's saying?" I kept walking.

"They know what virus you had." She curled her fingers and, when she started to throw my crew's hand sign, a bolt of adrenaline streaked through me.

I slapped her hands so fiercely my own fingers stung. Ariel had almost died earning the right to toss that sign. And Melissa had suffered worse. She still seemed more dead to me than alive.

"What?" Kaylee shook her hand.

"You don't have the right to throw that sign." My lips pressed together to keep me from saying worse.

"I was only kidding around," she said, hurt.

"It's not a joke," I snapped.

"I'm sorry. Okay?"

I glared at her, unable to accept her apology. She knew that kids our age and younger had died because they had flashed that sign.

"So I guess you didn't mean it when you said we'll always be friends," Kaylee shouted before she walked away and disappeared among the students who were watching the fight near the teachers' parking lot.

Calmly, coldly, I continued toward the school, my face intentionally blank. I had been ready to fight Kaylee. The thought sickened and surprised me. Maybe all the blows to my head during the jump-in had damaged my brain.

The kids studying on the front steps looked up from their books, their eyes quick and darting, afraid of me now that I was part of Core 9. They scooted and squeezed together, opening a gap for me while other students still had to wend their way around them.

Halfway up the stairs, I saw Dante with his wannabe crew, three nobodies, Vince, Tobias, and Justin, who were so anxious to get ganged up that they didn't bother to wonder why other Core 9 gangsters didn't hang out with Dante at school.

As I stepped closer, I realized that they had trapped Melissa and were jostling her from one to the other, touching her, and laughing at her attempts to slap their hands away. Why wasn't Dante afraid that Trek would come after him? His lack of fear chilled me. Dante knew the rules. As Trek's girlfriend, Melissa should have been off limits. Why wasn't she?

I grabbed a coffee from a skinny girl and hurled it at Dante. *Whack!* The lid snapped open and coffee splattered the back of his head. He spun around, fists ready to fight, his scowl dissolving when he saw me. He flicked his hand and his crew released Melissa.

She ran inside, her arms wrapped around her chest, head bowed, too ashamed to look at me.

"Melissa, wait!" I charged up the last steps, chasing after her.

"Hey, Blaise, why are you in such a hurry?" Dante teased as he braced his hands on either side of the doorjamb, his legs astraddle, like a six-year-old bully, his body blocking the entrance. "Did you want to go inside?"

His friends separated and started to encircle me.

"What's the matter, pretty face?" Dante asked.

I stared at him, not moving. Being part of Core 9 gave me prestige, but I had built my own reputation for toughness—a fighter who never backed down. If I let Dante and his wannabes stop me from going inside, then others might think they could challenge me, and I'd have to start fighting all over again to prove that I couldn't be pushed around.

"Well?" Dante asked, taunting me. "What are you waiting for?"

A wicked smile came to my lips as dormant memories awakened. Hadn't my mother taught me how to take down a guy without using my fists? I brushed back my hair, mimicking her, and let my hand slide down my neck to the top button on my blouse. My fingers lingered, a tease, then I tilted my head and undid the button. I laughed at the bewildered look on Dante's face. I could feel him drawn to me. No one had ever seen the vamp inside me. I kept her chained because I didn't want to be like my mother.

"Dante, I've wanted to talk to you for a while," I lied in a sugary voice.

"You have?" He looked completely disarmed.

"Of course I have." Did I actually giggle?

With a nod, he motioned his friends to back away. Vince and Justin paused and glanced at him, unsure, then looked at me, but Tobias prowled closer, his fingers twitching, wanting to grab me and hold me for the others.

I ignored him and focused my charm on Dante. "You avoid me," I complained prettily while stepping closer. "Whenever you see me, you always take off. Even at Trek's house."

"I don't," he protested, his sharp cologne stinging my nose.

"You do." I pouted, slipping my purse, heavy with the weight of the hammer, off my shoulder. I held the strap and sauntered closer, mirroring my mother's slow, sensual stride.

His defenses fell and longing filled his eyes.

I smoothed my right hand down his arm as my left hand swung forward and slammed my purse into his crotch. He gasped and fell to his knees and didn't have enough air left in his lungs to curse me.

His friends stared at him, then at me, too stunned to attack, while behind us, laughter burst into the air, followed by applause from the girls on the steps who had gathered to watch. Most had been victims of Dante's hallway attacks.

I looked at him now, on his knees, and wondered how he'd ever gotten into Core 9, then I pressed my face against the side of his head, my mouth at his ear. "If you touch Melissa again," I whispered, "your friends will have to scrape your body off the ground with butter knives."

When I sensed Tobias steeling himself to jump me, I pulled the hammer from my purse. "Try me," I said, facing him. "I'll make you pay for what you did."

"She's crazy. Leave her alone," Vince said, rescuing Tobias from what was going to be a crushing embarrassment.

"You think you're a guy," Dante said spitefully, still on his knees. "That's what everyone says."

I whipped around, so angry I had to restrain myself from biting his ear. "If I wanted you, I could still have you. But I don't, because I despise you for being such a fool."

Then, knocking into his shoulder, I shoved past him, hating the doubts that his words had released. I could be mean and aggressive like a guy, but had I also lost my compassion? I didn't want to be the person who provoked fear in others. Or did I? The only alternative was to become one of those girls who cried in the bathroom because someone had bullied her and taken her purse, or her homework, or her pride.

I avoided the security check, which was a fiasco with only one guard left to operate the metal detector, and wandered through the noisy, crowded hallway, no longer marveling at the way other students stepped out of my way.

I tried to call Melissa. I knew she'd found her phone, so why wasn't she answering? Finally, I texted, *call ME*.

Near my English class, Satch leaned against the wall, a trio of girls vying for his attention. Pretty girls with pink fingernails and hands that had never been bruised throwing punches. Looking at them, I wondered if Satch saw me as one of the guys.

As if he sensed me watching him, he glanced up. Waving, he broke away from the giggling trio and came over to me.

"Glad to have you back," he said as he squeezed me against him.

I closed my eyes and breathed in his scent, trying to analyze his touch. Was he holding me like a guy friend or a girl? I pulled back and glanced up. The way Satch was looking down at me sent a jolt through my stomach.

Turning away from him, I stared out at the crowded hallway. "So where's Rico?" I asked, nervously aware of Satch's fingers rubbing my back.

"Hey, Toughness," he teased. "Was my welcome not good enough?"

"I just thought he'd be here," I said, wondering what I'd felt inside me.

"We might not see him until later," Satch said, his hands dropping to his sides. "He's been going deeper into the Lobos' neighborhood and messing with their *placas*."

I waited, knowing there was more.

Satch pulled out his cell phone and a slide show began. "Some nights Rico stays in their neighborhood so he can catch their expressions when they discover what he's done."

I tried to block the fear rising inside me, but the foreboding came, stronger than ever. "They're going to catch him," I said. "There's no way they won't. We've got to stop him."

"I talked to him," Satch said, hiding his emotions, which I knew had to be volatile; he and Rico were closer than most brothers. "He says it's the only way he has to calm the anger inside him."

When the school day ended, I broke through the mob of students and headed across the field where band members had gathered for practice. Tubas, flutes, and clarinets piped out scales while drummers tapped a fast pace on their donated snare drums.

I pressed my cell phone against one ear and plugged my finger into the other, trying to hear Ariel. "Say it again and louder."

"I wish I could have come to school today," Ariel said. "What was it like?"

"Everyone treated me like royalty, but school's not fun without you. When are you coming back?"

"As soon as the headaches—"

My phone went dead. I had drained the battery with my attempts to reach Melissa. No one knew where she'd gone, and she hadn't answered my calls. That worried me. Maybe I'd find her at Trek's. I had to go there anyway, to feed the dogs. But first, I needed to pick up their food at Tulley's, which carried some staples along with the liquor.

I hiked down the alley as the beat of drums cracked the cool air and the band began to play. Four blocks later, near Tulley's, I could still hear the music, which almost drowned out the heavy steps of Satch and Rico trampling the gravel behind me.

"You should have waited for us," Rico scolded when they caught up to me. Black paint stained his fingers.

"Tulley's is too close to the Borderlands for you to come here alone," Satch added.

"Why do I suddenly need an escort?" I asked.

Their worried looks boomeranged from one to the other.

"A bunch of dopers were on your porch last night," Rico said.

"What's new with that?" I asked. "You've seen dopers in my yard before."

The homeless from the Borderlands came out every night and prowled around our neighborhood, scavenging for things they could sell to get money for drugs.

Rico opened the screen door, which had duct-tape patches over the holes. "Just be careful," he warned.

"I always am." I stepped inside and breathed in the scent of apples that were stacked in a crate next to the empty captain's chair where Mr. Tulley rested when he didn't have customers.

At the moment, he stood by the cash register in front of the cage that held cigarettes. When he saw me, he took his false teeth off the counter, placed them in his mouth, and worked his lips to settle the dentures onto his gums.

"You don't have to put your teeth in for us," Satch said.

"I'm not trying to look handsome for you, Satch," Mr. Tulley said. "I'm wearing my teeth for Blaise." He tapped his bandaged fingers on the cans of dog food that were stacked next to a bag of kibble.

"Filet mignon." Satch read a label. "Pixie and Bonnie eat better than we do."

"Pit bulls should not be called Pixie and Bonnie," a voice came from behind us. "I got love for you, Blaise, but those names are a humiliation."

I spun around.

Danny stood stock-still, not looking the least bit afraid, a liter of Coke in one hand and a bag of pizza-flavored chips in the other. I gaped at the Egyptian cross that swung from a chain around his neck. Had Ariel given him her silver ankh necklace?

Grinning, Satch edged closer to the captain's chair and blocked the exit aisle, his fingers clenching, while Rico inched forward, his breath slow and deep, the sharp scent of adrenaline coming off him.

Danny's smile turned Cheshire and, the moment Satch and Rico lunged for him, he hurdled over the captain's chair and apple crate and landed in a graceful run. His body hit the screen door and he tore outside, dropping the Coke and chips on the porch.

Satch and Rico raced after him, their feet battering the warped floor. The wooden boards creaked and rocked, the motion shaking the shelves until the bottles rattled against each other.

I grabbed the sack of dog food, leaving the change for Mr. Tulley, and dashed outside in time to see Satch throw himself into a dive, his hands grasping for Danny's ankles.

Sensing the tackle, Danny loped to the right, into the stubby weeds. Satch landed flat on his stomach, his fingers skimming over the backs of Danny's tennis shoes, as Danny bounded onto the Oldsmobile parked at the curb, his weight setting off the *bleeps* of the theft alarm. He crossed the hood, jumped into the street, and ran toward a bicycle that leaned against a tree.

"Stay down!" Rico shouted when Satch started to get up.

Rico leaped over Satch, onto the Olds. The metal popped and twanged as he darted over the car roof and flung himself onto the street, hitting the pavement close to Danny, who jerked his shoulders and flinched away.

With a burst of speed, Danny dashed forward, his feet slamming the ground faster than I'd ever seen anyone run. He grabbed the handlebars on the bike, swung his leg over the seat, and peddled away, pulling a wheelie.

Rico walked back to us, frowning, his chest heaving, as Satch stood and brushed off his clothes, looking sullen.

From the corner of my eye, I saw movement behind Tulley's screen door and turned quickly enough to catch a hazy image of Ariel, who stared back at me before she edged deeper into the store. An uneasy feeling crawled into my stomach and settled in for a long stay. What would Satch and Rico have done if they had caught her with Danny? What would I have been forced to do?

By the time we'd reached Trek's house, I had stopped chewing on the inside of my mouth and, though Rico and Satch had been talking, I wouldn't have been able to repeat a word they'd said, because my thoughts had been so focused on Ariel. How could she put herself in such danger for a guy?

Omar greeted us, alone on the porch, and blocked our way. His hands skidded down Satch, then Rico, checking for guns, before he frisked me. Satisfied we were clean, he opened the door and let us inside. The moment I stepped into the living room, my body stiffened. The atmosphere was heavy with tension.

I glanced at Dante, who looked away, intentionally avoiding my gaze.

Trek sat in one of the chrome-armed chairs and stared at me, not smiling the way he usually did when I came over to feed the dogs. Though he was probably furious with me for humiliating Dante, in my opinion, he should have been thanking me.

Satch spread out on the couch while Rico leaned against the wall.

"Is Melissa here?" I asked as Bonnie and Pixie raced out of the kitchen, their hind ends wagging.

"She's shopping," Trek said, curtly.

I didn't need to see his look to know he wanted me to leave the room. I herded the puppies, who'd outgrown their box, back to the kitchen, set my purse and the sack of food near the sink, and listened as I bent down and petted the dogs, who mewled against me, hungry.

"I hope you two are here to tell me you got Danny," Trek said.

"We missed him again," Satch replied. "We'll get him eventually, but if you want your money back, we're cool with that."

"Did I say I wanted my money back?" Trek asked. "What I want is Danny with a busted head."

"And you'll get it," Rico said emphatically.

"When you go on a mission," Trek countered, "if you don't make the nightly news, then you didn't do the job that you were sent out to do."

"Are you saying we didn't try hard enough?" Rico asked defensively.

"Why would you think that?" Trek asked with a curious calmness in his voice. "You know you're my favorites. You'd never let me down, would you, Rico?"

I peeled the lid off a can, scooped the dog food into a bowl, and set it on the floor, the meaty-garlic smell saturating the air, as the voices in the living room became hushed.

When the whispers stopped, I figured they had reached an impasse.

Finally, Trek's voice broke the silence. "Dante, give them a gun."

Air left my lungs in a rush of fear. I knew they didn't want to shoot Danny, but my worry flipped to Ariel. Would she be standing next to him when they fired?

After a pause, Satch spoke. "We can shoot Danny, but getting shot is too random in this neighborhood. No one will see it as a warning. Some other hustler will slide in where Danny left off. It's like you said in the beginning; Danny with a broken nose is a walking billboard, warning others not to move in on your territory."

"Satch, you think too much," Rico complained. "Trek's got the right idea. We're never going to catch Danny. Let's just shoot him. It's easier."

"Wait," Trek warned.

"Give me the gun. I'll do it." Rico's eagerness was a bluff to plant doubt in Trek's mind, because he hated what Lobos called *locura*, the craziness that made some homies too quick to react. Trek liked to strategize, plan, and wait. For him, the game was more exciting than the victory.

Trek said, "No gun. We'll go back to my original plan."

Dante finally spoke. "How are they going to catch him?"

"We need a lure," Trek said. "A girl who can distract Danny and make him careless."

"Melissa can do it," Dante suggested.

"Any fool knows she can't be the lure," Trek said, annoyed. "How is she going to lure anyone when everyone knows she's with me?"

"I'm just saying, she could if—"

"She's not a possibility." Trek cut him off, and then to Satch and Rico, he said, "I'll find someone and get back to you."

Satch and Rico left in silence through the front door, while in the living room Trek spoke to Dante in a low grumble that told me he was upset with him.

Good, I thought. I hoped he kicked Dante out on the street for what he'd done to Melissa.

I spread clean newspapers over the floor, anxious to catch up to Satch and Rico and, as I started to stand, I glanced at the floorboard. Several scratches nicked the wood. Had they been there before?

Quickly, I refilled the water bowl and set it down, then crouched beside the dogs. While they lapped the water, my gaze drifted back to the scratches, which looked new. Had someone broken into Trek's stash? My thoughts settled on Rico. He wouldn't, surely he wouldn't—but my heart dropped because I knew he would.

Fighting the urge to look behind the wall and see if the drugs were still there, I jumped up and collided into Trek, who had been standing over me.

"Sorry," I said, stepping back. "I didn't hear you come into the kitchen."

"That's because I didn't want you to hear me." He touched the side of my neck, his fingers resting on my pulsing vein. "Your heart's racing. Have I made you nervous about something?"

"No, of course not." My voice sounded labored.

He stared at me, his eyes unreadable. I lifted my chin in defiance. Did he think I was stealing from him?

"I have a job for you," he said at last. "I want you to be my lure."

"Me?" I laughed in disbelief. "A lure has to be sexy, like Melissa." *Like my mother.* "Guys on the street don't even give me a second look."

"That's because you never give them anything to look at. You hide yourself in baggy clothes."

"I can't lure anyone. I don't have that special power," I said, reasoning that if I had my mother's magic, guys would be flocking around me. "No one is going to get careless looking at me."

"Dante did. The 3Ts bragged about the way you handled him this morning. Tara said you're a natural."

"Did anyone tell you why I attacked him?" I asked, the memory curdling my stomach.

"Melissa did. She laughed about it."

"She laughed?" I blinked against the confusion and doubt that were rising inside me.

"She was teasing Dante and having fun. Some girls like to play."

"That doesn't sound like Melissa," I argued. "She—" I'd almost said *hates Dante* but held back. I could hear him prowling in the next room and I didn't want him to give her more trouble.

"Melissa isn't upset about this, so why are you?" Trek asked, frowning.

"I didn't like what I saw. It looked wrong."

"Maybe you *saw wrong*," Trek suggested.

I took deep breaths, trying to stay calm. Had Melissa been playing with Dante and his crew, only ashamed when I caught her? I stifled the cry in my throat. My mother had liked to play.

"You don't need to protect Melissa. I'll take care of her." Trek rubbed my arm, soothing me, before he took my hand. "Come on. I'm going to prove to you that you're beautiful."

He led me into the laundry room. When I saw the full-length mirror, I ducked around him and tried to escape. His hands caught my hips, forcing me to turn and face my reflection.

I stared at the floor, unable to look, sweat erupting under my arms, prickling with the intensity of my nervousness.

"Why do you act like beauty's a crime?" he asked from behind me.

"I don't," I sputtered. Images of my mother streaked through my mind.

"Watch." His hands lifted my chin, then smoothed down my

neck to my shoulders, his fingers collecting the collar of my gray cardigan, which he pulled off my arms.

I shivered, my skin clammy, and glanced down, confused for a moment, as he undid my skirt button.

"What are you . . . ?" I was trembling.

"I'm showing you what you hide." He slid the zipper down.

I caught his hand, his fingers warm in my icy, sweating palm.

"Don't you trust me?" he asked. "You've come over to my house every day, alone, and nothing's happened."

"I trust you. It's that . . ."

"You act like you're afraid to let me see your beauty," he said softly.

"Beauty," I sniffed, not glancing at my reflection. "All you're going to see is my ratty underwear."

"All right, then," he said, his voice suddenly impatient. He took his hand away and my skirt slipped below my hipbones, the torn elastic on my panties sliding into view.

Heat rose to my face. "I told you," I whispered.

"You need to see yourself as I see you," he scolded. He lifted my chin again, and this time I relented and looked in the mirror, my breath coming in swatches.

Still standing behind me, he unbuttoned my blouse and let it fall open, my breasts bulging against the tight-fitting, second-hand bra. "Why do you hide yourself?"

"Because." I glanced at the mirror. I saw my mother in my reflection, the perfect body and huge round eyes under arched brows, though mine had never been plucked. I licked the lips that looked like hers, full and deep in color even without lipstick. Tears clung to my black lashes. Everyone had said that she could have been a model if she hadn't gotten pregnant with me at fifteen.

"One glance at you and any guy will fall," Trek said against my ear.

"Blaise!" Satch's voice startled me. "What's taking so long?"

My heart raced. When had he come inside? He burst into the laundry room and saw my reflection, his mouth opening, confusion on his face. Satch had never even seen me in a bathing suit, and never this way with a guy . . . with Trek, who was smiling broadly.

"Blaise is going to be the lure," Trek said, arrogantly assuming I would do it. He grabbed my limp arms, my skirt falling to my ankles as he turned me until I faced Satch, who tensed his jaw.

"She can't," Satch said, his knuckles punching the doorjamb. "She's just a kid."

Trek stepped in front of me, his eyes scanning my body. I gasped for air as the room swayed. He grabbed my arm to steady me. "She doesn't look like a kid to me."

I stared at the floor, then back at Satch, who argued, "Trek, you know damn well what I mean. Get a girl who knows something about guys."

"Blaise is the one I chose," Trek said abruptly.

Satch's gaze held mine, a vein pulsing in his temple. He probably thought I'd never be able to lure a guy. He frowned and looked away, no doubt trying to figure out a way to tell Trek he'd made a mistake in choosing me. *Blaise is a fighter*, I

103

imagined him saying. *She doesn't know how to charm a guy. She thinks she is one.*

Staring into the kitchen, Satch swallowed hard. "Rico and I'll be waiting for you on the corner."

His steps quickened, pounding into thunder. Then the back door slammed, shaking the house and setting off the wind chimes in a cacophony of clatter and jangles and clanks.

Nearly tripping over my skirt, which hobbled my feet, I faced Trek and shoved him hard. "I can't do it," I said. "How can I lure someone in my school uniform? That's the best I own. I wear the hand-me-downs that the churchwomen give my grandmother."

I looked at Trek and energy passed between us, a sadness of understanding, as if he had known deep poverty and had once felt its shame. The moment passed so quickly, I thought it had to be my imagination, until he spoke. "I don't want you to ever feel like you're second best." He reached into his pocket and pulled out a roll of bills that he pressed into my palm. "Tell those church-women to find another charity. You buy your own clothes from now on, pretty things to match your face. No more hiding in sec-ondhand clothes."

I stared down at the money, knowing I should give it back, but I couldn't, because it felt too good in my hand.

I stepped outside, into the blinding light, the late afternoon filled with the squeals from children who had stolen the police tape off a crime scene and were running with it clutched in their uplifted hands, the yellow ribbons streaming behind them. They rushed into the park, over the newly seeded grass, where burnt leaves swirled off the trees and scattered around them before spinning over me.

When the leaves settled, I saw Satch and Rico and lifted my head, scowling to hide my embarrassment as I remembered how Satch had seen me with Trek.

Rico met me and picked the leaves from my hair. His fingers lingered, caressing my face. "Trek didn't explain everything to you," he said, the patronizing tone in his voice irritating me. "It's dangerous what he's asking."

"So is walking to school," I countered, squeezing around him. "I wouldn't be a gangster if I wanted to play safe. I'd be trying to snag a guy and end up pregnant before I finished high school, and then live off welfare and part-time jobs. I want more than crying babies and swollen ankles, and that requires risk."

"Blaise." Rico stretched my name into three syllables to show me he didn't like my response, which only annoyed me more. "If the guy you're luring gets suspicious, you'll be the first target."

I whipped around. "Where do you think I've been living? I've been a target all my life."

"You can't do this," he said, more strongly now.

"Did I say I was going to?" I broke away from him and glanced at Satch, who trudged behind us. His silence irked me. Was it so impossible for him to imagine me as a lure? I clenched the money and hurried away, furious with Rico for arguing with me and just as mad at Satch for not.

Rico chased after me. "So you told Trek no?"

"He just asked me. I haven't decided." I plodded forward, my heavy steps expressing my agitation. I needed time alone to think.

"How can you even consider it?" Rico caught up to me.

"The money," I said. "What other reason could there be?"

"I can give you money." He had offered this before. "Everything I have is yours. Tell me how much you want. I've got plenty now."

"You need what you have. You're already supporting your mother." I drew back, skirting around him, and bumped into Satch, whose hands clamped my shoulders and forced me to stay still as he moved in front of me.

"You're tough," Satch said, "but you're not tough enough to do what Trek's going to expect from you." His hands fell to his sides. "The danger doesn't stop after you've lured a guy."

"After I've lured a guy? What? You think I could?" I held his gaze for a long moment.

"Of course I do," he said, glancing sideways at Rico. "Only a fool wouldn't be attracted to you."

Excitement shivered through me, but before I could reflect on what he had said, Rico barged between us.

"A guy who is beaten because you distracted him is going to remember how he got caught," Rico said. "And when he recovers, he'll come after you, and it won't be a quick revenge. You've heard the stories."

I nodded, my mood dampened. "But Danny . . . he wouldn't."

"What makes you think Trek's only going to use you for Danny?" Satch asked as we stopped in front of my grandmother's house.

I had no answer.

Rico drew in a deep breath, revving up to give me a lecture, but Satch spoke first. "We won't catch Danny on our own. So it's on you. Is that what you want, Danny with his face smashed in?"

"No." I clenched my purse strap. "But don't put it on me. If I don't lure him, Trek will find someone else. So what's the difference? You're not going to get out of beating him if I say no."

"You're going to do this, aren't you?" Rico said with unpleasant coldness.

"Maybe."

He picked up a discarded beer bottle and threw it across the street. The glass shattered against the curb, shards rattling down the gutter. He turned back, his words seething through his teeth.

"If you do this, then I'm looking at a dead girl. How long do you think you'll last?"

"We all have to go sometime." I responded with the gangster's mantra before I hurried to the porch, leaving them with their unfinished lectures.

Without making a sound, I went inside and glanced back at the street. Satch and Rico had already left. A familiar heaviness weighed on my heart. Their quick departure told me they weren't going to get over this easily. Maybe they never would. Quietly, I shut the door, the money still scrunched in my hand.

I started toward the kitchen and was surprised to see my grandmother at the table, her back to me, palms upturned, her focus too deep in prayer to have heard me come in. I tiptoed closer, listening to her murmur while I stared at the medical bills spread in front of her. How many doctors was she seeing? Even with Medicare, the amount she owed, highlighted in yellow, was staggering.

Next to the stack of bills was an overdue notice from the mortgage company. She had told me that the house payment was more than her social security check, but I had never imagined it could have been that much higher. A mortgage banker had taken advantage of her, convinced her that she could manage the payment and, when she couldn't, the bank had charged her ridiculously high late fees.

I saw her struggle in the long column of withdrawals on the statement for my college fund. She had tried to keep her dream of sending me to college a reality by taking out only a little money at a time. Even so, she had almost depleted the account.

I placed the money that Trek had given me on the table in front of her. "I love you, Grandma," I said.

She flinched, her smile faltering as her eyes tracked down to the money and, then, back to me. "Where did you get this?"

"I told you about my job looking after the dogs," I said.

She counted the money, pressing each bill flat. When she finished, she frowned, her face besieged with doubt. "Five hundred dollars is too much for feeding dogs."

The amount staggered me.

"Where'd you get so much money?"

"Trek," I said.

"He gets his money in a bad way," she countered.

There was no use lying. The truth seemed suddenly stronger. "Trek is the only way I have to help you."

"Then don't." Her frown deepened as her finger tapped the money. "You take this back."

"I can't," I said in a low voice. "I won't."

Her eyes widened slightly to hear me defy her, but she no longer had the strength she'd once had to scold me into a corner.

I continued, "If you don't stop working, you'll be dead in less than a year and, without you, I'll end up living with my mother. Would you want that?"

"You know I wouldn't." She shook her head.

"Then let me help you the only way I can. Please."

She wiped the edges of her eyes. I had given her an impossible choice, between Trek and my mother.

"I promise I'm not doing anything wrong," I lied this time to be kind. "I'm just working for Trek."

"This isn't fair to you, baby," she whispered. "Isn't fair and isn't right. If I were stronger—"

"But you're not." I shushed her. "So you have to let me do this. It's just a job like any other. I'm not getting involved in the bad stuff. I promise. But Trek's got money and he's generous."

I could feel her giving in, and slowly the shaking of her head turned into a nod. I pulled her to me. I could barely feel the weight of her arms and knew I'd made the right decision.

"Let me finish out the month," she bargained. "Maybe we can catch up on the bills, sell the house, and move."

"One month," I agreed, to give her hope, though I didn't know how she could manage that long. "And then you quit your job. You've sacrificed everything for me, and it's time to let me take care of you."

"Thank you, baby," she whispered, choking on the words. "It's been hard. I couldn't even get all my floors cleaned last night."

Her gratitude absolved me of any shame. If Danny had to live the rest of his life with a crooked nose so my grandmother could stay home and enjoy the limited days she had left, then so be it. Ariel might never forgive me. And Satch and Rico were never going to understand—but in that moment, holding my grandmother while she cried, I had decided to become the lure.

16

I had outgrown the color pink but still lived with it ruffled around my room. A year ago, in desperation, I had painted one wall yellow with old paint I'd found in the garage. The pink had seeped through, leaving a lurid, pulsating orange that Ariel had promised to cover with a mural. Tonight, she was blocking out the figures while I sat on my bed, watching her. She had sketched four girls across my bedroom wall, their faces divided with lines as she worked on their expressions. I was, without doubt, the angry one.

"Why did Melissa want us to meet here?" Ariel asked, checking the time on her cell phone. She had dressed as if she was going on a mission: long-sleeved black T-shirt, work shoes and jeans, no false eyelashes.

"She told me it was a surprise," I replied, wondering why Ariel had said nothing about Danny. Did she think I hadn't seen her inside Tulley's?

She returned to her drawing, her charcoal stick scratching the wall. "I can't stay much longer."

"Why?" I asked. "Are you meeting someone?"

"I have to—"

"Where's that Egyptian cross you bought for protection?" I demanded.

She shrugged. "Lost it, I guess."

"In Tulley's liquor store?"

The charcoal screeched under the pressure of her fingers before it shattered.

"Friends don't keep secrets from each other," I said.

Ariel picked up the charcoal fragments and started packing her pencils into a canvas tote. "I'm not keeping secrets, I'm *keeping* you safe," she said without looking up. "I'm not telling you anything in case I'm found out. There's no reason for both of us to get killed."

"And death is the best outcome, isn't it? Because worse things happen to girls in our neighborhood. Is any guy worth the risk?"

"Danny is," she responded in a low voice as the door opened downstairs.

"I'm sorry I'm late!" Melissa yelled, barging inside.

Ariel looked up, surprised. "She sounds happy. Could she be?"

We stood motionless, waiting, and I realized we were both hoping to hear her sing. Finally, we walked down the hallway to meet her.

"Surprise!" Melissa yelled, carrying an assortment of shopping bags that rustled against her jeans as she raced up the stairs. "I would have been here hours ago, but it took me forever to pick out the right clothes and makeup for you, Blaise." She breezed past us, acting bubbly, but her eyes had a hollowness that sent a shudder through me.

"We need to get started," Melissa continued. "Trek said I have to transform you into a lure, and that could take all night."

"A lure?" Ariel whipped around, her eyes sparking with suspicion when she looked at me. "Who are you supposed to set up?"

"Trek wants her to go after Danny," Melissa said from my bedroom.

Ariel shoved me against the wall, her arm jammed into the base of my neck. "Is that why you were asking so many questions?"

I sputtered, my throat gurgling. I didn't fight back, though I knew I could win, because that victory would cost me our friendship.

Melissa heard me gag and glanced over her shoulder. Dropping the bags, she rushed back and pulled Ariel off me. "What's that about?"

"Friends don't keep secrets from each other," Ariel said, her words punching the air.

"She didn't tell me either," Melissa said, holding on to Ariel. "Trek did. I mean, look at her. Is she sexy enough to make a guy forget he's got enemies? There's no way she could have believed Trek was serious. That's why she didn't say anything."

Looking me up and down, Ariel's anger vanished. "Sorry."

I hadn't thought Trek was making fun of me, but I let them believe I had. I said nothing and rubbed my neck, annoyed at both my friends.

As Melissa headed back to my room, Ariel pressed her face against my ear. "You'll warn me if you really do go after Danny, right?"

"Of course," I lied, hoping she'd fall out of love with him before I had to do anything. If they had a bad enough split, maybe she'd even be happy to see him with a busted nose.

"I can't stay," Ariel said, snooping around the makeup and brushes that Melissa was setting out on my desk. She stuck a lipstick up her sleeve, grabbed her tote, and headed for the hallway.

"I saw you," Melissa yelled after her.

"I knew you would." Ariel laughed as she ran down the stairs.

"Did she really think I wouldn't see her take the lipstick?" Melissa asked, pulling the chair away from my desk and motioning for me to sit.

"You bought two," I said, the chair legs squeaking under me. "That's like an invitation."

"Ariel's the reason I had to buy two," Melissa said defensively before she ran a comb through my hair. She grabbed a pair of scissors from her pile of beauty tools and, without looking at me, said, "So tell me all about it. I want to hear every detail. How did Trek choose you? You must have been thrilled." She tried to sound casual, but I could hear the jealous strain in her voice.

"I'm sure you were his first choice," I said, wondering if she had grown so dependent on Trek that she was fearful of losing him. "But there's no way he could use you when everyone knows you're a couple."

"I suppose." The scissors snipped across my forehead and,

after all the clumps of hair had settled on my lap, she lifted my chin and examined her work, the tips of the blades dangerously close to my eyes. "Trek said you were a natural, but how could he know unless—?"

"Melissa!" Had Trek purposefully tried to make her jealous? He must have. "Tara told Trek I was a natural after she watched me take down Dante."

Smiling slightly, Melissa seemed to relax. "I heard about the way you slammed him to his knees." She appeared pleased that I had.

"Were you just playing around with Dante?" I ventured, watching her closely. "You know, having fun, when I interfered?"

She drew in a ragged breath. "I'm okay with Dante."

But I didn't see okay in her eyes. I saw hate. Even so, I didn't push her, because I sensed she was still too fragile. Had Dante been one of the nine? I couldn't remember.

"I'm going to keep him away from you anyway," I vowed.

She paused, staring at nothing, and I thought she'd muttered "thank you," though I wasn't sure. When she finally turned back, she forced a smile and held up a pair of tweezers. "This is going to hurt."

"Ouch!" She hadn't lied. I leaned back and grimaced as she plucked my brows.

While she did my makeup and curled my hair, she talked about Trek, her voice sometimes rising to a tightness that made me think she was going to cry, but I didn't see tears until we stood in front of my grandmother's mirror, breathing the fusty smell of a bedroom that never saw sunlight.

"Wow," she whispered. I could tell she was comparing our faces. I had never been her competition before. "Trek was right," she said slowly, her tone hard to read. "You look incredible."

Finally, I glanced at my reflection and took in a sharp breath, my stomach twisting. I looked like my mother, the startlingly beautiful girl who had been homecoming queen and snow princess and my father's girlfriend. I lifted my hand and waved, testing to make sure I was really seeing me.

"Come on," Melissa said. "Trek wanted to check you out after I finished."

"Not tonight," I said, self-conscious. No one had ever seen me dressed like this, so brazenly exposed. I was wearing lacy underwear, softer than any I'd ever owned, a sleek blue dress that slithered over my body, and stiletto heels that killed my toes. "I'm not ready."

Melissa sat on my grandmother's bed and let out a slow, quiet sigh. "Blaise, if you don't go with me, Trek will think I didn't want him to see you." She looked up at me. "Please. Let me show you off."

I hesitated.

"Satch and Rico won't be at the party, if that's what's got you worried. They're collecting some money for Trek." She waited and then added, "Please do this for me."

I pushed my modesty aside and held out my hand. "Let's go."

"Thanks." Her sudden smile warmed me.

I grabbed my key and followed her outside, where I kept glancing at the dark houses, fearful a neighbor would see me marching down the street half-naked.

As we passed Tulley's, I could hear the music blasting from Tara's house. Dogs howled in pain from the ear-piercing sounds that didn't seem to bother the guys leaning against the cars parked on the lawn.

Unaware of how deep my embarrassment actually was, Melissa led me up the walk, past the homeboys who followed us inside where the hot, moist air felt gluey after the cold.

Beneath my feet, the floor trembled from the music pounding out of the speakers, the vibration quivering up my body. I breathed in the smoke, my stomach jittery and, as my eyes adjusted to the dim light, I felt hands brushing over me, touching my hair and arms. Guys who usually ignored me crushed around me, candlelight illuminating their faces. I could see their desire and sensed it, too, as they asked my name, trying to talk to me over the loud music. No one even recognized me.

I was expecting Melissa to show me how to handle so many guys, but she was breathing jaggedly, her eyes wide and empty. Some of the homeboys pushing against us had been part of the nine who had taken her upstairs the night of the *rollins*.

Holding her protectively against me, I guided her to Trek, who stood near a line of candles, his glossy hair down and flowing over his shoulders. He kissed Melissa, enfolding her into his arms, and let her relax against him. I wondered if he had seen her fear—and if he had, why hadn't he come to rescue her?

"Perfect," Trek declared, eyeing me appraisingly. Then to Melissa he said, "Take Blaise back to the 3Ts and show them what you've done."

Her confidence restored, Melissa led me to the kitchen, where the smoke was thicker and burned my lungs. The homegirls were dancing with guys, their knees interlocked, while they kissed and pumped and laughed.

"What do you think of Blaise?" Melissa asked loudly. "Come check her out."

The homegirls broke away from their boyfriends and squeezed around me. My ears buzzed with words I had never expected to hear describing me.

I glanced at Melissa, who looked happy about all the praise I was receiving. She clung to me as if I were her life preserver, keeping her afloat. "I feel like every compliment you're receiving is really a compliment for me, since I'm the one who transformed you," Melissa whispered against my ear. "Maybe I'm good for something."

"You'll be our secret weapon, Blaise." Tara laughed. "You'll leave them defenseless and we'll leave them dead."

I stood stock-still as an ugly sensation slid through me, a mix of guilt and shame that left me queasy. I broke away from Melissa and, in the living room, wiggled my way through the homeboys who wanted to dance, their muscled bodies pressing against me.

On the porch, I kicked off my shoes, leaped onto the lawn, and raced into the cool night as a sob exploded from deep within me. I ran in the opposite direction of my home. I didn't want to go where Melissa and the others could find me. I needed the moon and the stars, and the possibility of a different life. I sprinted along the edge of the Borderlands, the silty ground squishing between my toes, and continued until I was exhausted.

I stopped in a patch of grass, my legs weak and trembling, and wiped the tears and sweat from my face. My hands came back streaked with makeup and one false eyelash, which looked like a dead caterpillar. I stared at it, feeling sorry for myself, and then with a sudden jolt, I scanned the shadows. I was no longer alone.

Though I saw no one, my gut told me I was being watched. I stared up at the windows of the abandoned row houses, searching for a face, until a soft rustle caught my attention. It could have been no more than windblown leaves and trash scratching down the gutter, but the noise set me on edge.

I became aware again of how little I was wearing and risked a look over my shoulder, my fatigued muscles tensing, ready to run, but there was only the sway of tree shadows, a speckled pattern of light and dark, spinning across the sidewalk.

Down the block, from behind an iron fence, came the scuff of heavy footsteps. I eased back into gauzy spider webs and waited, hidden beside a tree. The person kept coming, slow and confident, crunching over broken glass. The shards crackled and skittered, the noise taunting me, letting me know the person walking toward me felt no need for caution; I was easy prey and too close to the Borderlands for anyone to hear my screams.

My natural instinct was to run, but I didn't know who was there. Homeless dopers worked in packs. The footsteps might be an attempt to flush me out and force me to run into the waiting arms of others, who would grab me and carry me into an open basement.

Better to stay hidden and, if found, fight only one. I crouched down, my fingers searching over the spongy ground through moldered leaves, until I grasped a stick strong enough to gouge an eye.

The footsteps sounded less than a few yards away. I stood and waited, careful with my breathing, and then not breathing when the person paused. I lifted the stick, the muscles in my arms aching with the need to attack.

"Blaise?" From the other side of the tree, Trek strolled into view and stopped in front of me, his smile sly, the night breeze lifting his hair in a sensual caress.

I released my breath, my fear turning to rage. I wanted to jab the stick into the side of his perfect face, even though I sensed that he had only been testing me.

His hand slid down my arm, pried the stick from my hand, and tossed it into the street. "You've got the beauty and guts to take down anyone," he said. "Tomorrow you're going to lure Nando."

I started to laugh. He had to be joking. Everyone feared Nando, a hard-core Lobo.

When Trek didn't smile, my stomach clenched.

"When?" I whispered uneasily.

"Right after school."

Nando was legendary. Vicious. Violent. Cruel. He would never succumb to me.

I was a dead girl.

I sat in Trek's Mercedes, my hands clamped around the bottle of water he had given me. The plastic crackled when I took a sip. Even after three swallows, the metallic taste clung to my mouth.

"If you're tasting fear, water isn't going to get rid of it," Trek said as he steered the car past a storefront medical clinic that specialized in back pain.

"I wouldn't be nervous if you'd let me take my purse," I argued. "Nando has seen me around school. If he recognizes me, I'll need the hammer."

"He won't recognize you," Trek assured me. "I can guarantee it."

I glanced at my reflection in the side view mirror. I barely recognized myself in the feathery lashes and glossy lipstick. Melissa had volunteered to do my makeup again, her eagerness surprising me. She had brought over new spiky shoes and another blue dress, this one even shorter than the one I'd worn last night.

"Nando's hiding out in the corner building, first floor, last apartment," Trek said, pulling me back to the present. "He'll have set up some kind of alarm or trap, so be careful once you get inside."

The building looked deserted. The iron bars on the windows had rusted and bled over the bricks that years of automobile exhaust had encrusted with soot. Even the weeds sprouting from the cracks in the foundation had black grime on their leaves.

"The front door has a security lock," Trek continued. "You'll have to sneak in."

He caught me staring at his fighting shoes, Bulldog black Grinders with steel toes, the soles like tire tread. "I'm wearing the shoes so I can protect you," he said.

"You're not expecting this to be easy," I said.

"I wouldn't need you if it was going to be easy." Trek parked near the elementary school then, facing me, took the bottle of water and set it in the cup holder. "I won't let anything happen to you. I'll kill Nando if he touches you."

If he touches me? My heart thudded, warning me this was going to be worse than the disaster I was imagining. "Let me take my purse. I can handle anything with my hammer."

"The first thing Nando would do is check inside your purse, and if he sees a hammer, he'll know you're not a schoolgirl with a crush." Trek unsnapped my seatbelt. "Here they come."

Children dressed in beige and navy blue uniforms rushed from the school, papers rustling in their hands, their yells and shrieks rising as they jumped and batted at the pink magnolia petals falling around them.

I opened the car door, climbed out, and strolled toward the

corner, four inches taller in the stiletto heels, my silky dress clinging to my thighs, while the children jostled around me.

I waited in front of the building until three boys and two girls raced up the crumbling concrete steps. The oldest boy, eleven years old maybe, unlocked the door and, when I started inside, he gave me a smile filled with trust before he darted up the stairs after the other children, who were calling out the rules for their game of jailbreak hide-and-seek.

Using grocery flyers that were scattered over the entrance floor, I wedged the door open so Trek could get inside, then paused. The banister had broken free from the stairs and dangled from the top post, creaking softly over the entrance to the first floor hallway, the sticks missing from the swinging handrail, stolen for use as weapons or baseball bats or, perhaps, to create that impression. *A trap?* If I pushed the loose railing aside, it might collapse and fall on top of me, the noise warning Nando, telling him he had a visitor.

I eased around the drooping banister then, letting my eyes adjust to the dark, continued down the corridor, where water dripped on the lumpy carpet. The pungent smell of mildew mixed with the sour odor from rat nests hidden in the walls, but a third scent brought a smile to my face. From under the door of the end apartment, thin smoke hazed into the air. Nando was for sure mellow, maybe high, his reaction slowed. This was going to be easy after all.

I knocked and, before I could even take a pose, the door crashed open and banged against the wall, the boom shuddering through me. White light exploded in my eyes, then streaked behind me.

"Where's Trek?" Nando pointed a gun at me and tossed the searchlight aside. It clattered on the floor and sent shadows sliding over the walls.

Fear overwhelmed me, the onslaught so strong I couldn't breathe. I gazed into Nando's eyes, which were as green and clear and intense as those of the wolf tattooed on his neck. Nando wasn't high, not even mellow. A dish filled with smoldering leaves sat next to the door, a subterfuge to make his attacker as careless as I had been.

"How'd Trek find me?" He latched his arm around me and forced me against his powerfully built body, the gun barrel jabbing my temple. "Who gave me up?"

"I wanted to meet you," I yelled. "I—"

"Trek!" Nando shouted over my words. He pressed my face into his chest, his scent strong of aftershave, oranges, and cigarettes. "I got your bitch!"

If Trek stood in the shadows, he remained silent. The only sounds came from the dripping water and the whispering children, whose small steps scuffed down the stairs as they searched for a hiding place.

Nando jerked the gun away from my head and fired toward the entrance, the muzzle flash lighting the hallway. The recoil jolted his shoulder and knocked through me.

In the ringing silence that followed, images of dead children rose from my well of memories. I grabbed the gun barrel, my anger too fierce to allow caution, and caught Nando off guard. Because he held the gun with only one hand, I took it from him easily, then jumped back into safe firing range, the handle grip slick with his sweat.

"Kids were on the staircase." The words scraped up my burning throat. "If your recklessness killed a kid, then I'm going to be reckless, too. And after you're dead, I'll drop the gun and walk away. No one will even care until your corpse becomes an insufferable stink."

The blast must have deafened him as it had me and, though he couldn't hear my threat, he could see the malice in my eyes. He appraised me, his sinuous arms twitching.

Slowly, my hearing returned. A little boy was crying. A girl, maybe his sister, tried to comfort him while the other children urged them both up the stairs, their need to hide no longer a game. But no one was dead. No one was shot.

My full attention turned to Nando, whose smug grin warned me that I only had seconds before he tried to jump me. *Where was Trek?* I had to assume that he hadn't been able to get inside, or worse, had taken the bullet fired into the dark. Either way, I had to leave.

"I've wanted to meet you for a long time," I lied. And taking a gamble, I clicked on the safety in front of the trigger guard and held the gun at my side.

Nando's shoulders sagged, the motion slight, but enough to let me know he had believed me capable of firing.

"I finally got up the courage to knock on your door and for

what? I should have stayed home and watched TV." I strutted away with a sensual roll of my hips, my pace slow though my heart *thwacked* its beats in a painful rhythm, impatient for me to run.

Nando didn't chase after me. My gun skills had left him with enough doubt to worry that I might be leading him to an ambush. At the same time, he didn't want to lose me. I sensed his dilemma when he called, "Don't go. I'm sorry."

"Sorry you were going to kill me?" I pouted without looking back, but I liked the plea I had heard in his voice. Could this be working?

"Come back."

"Forget it. I'm not interested now." When I neared the end of the hallway, Trek slipped from the shadows, his steps as silent as air. He nodded, motioning me back to Nando, who was still coaxing me to return to him.

"Let's talk," Nando said. "I really am sorry."

I spun around, my smile huge and forgiving. "You're truly sorry?"

"Truly," he breathed.

I strolled back to him and played shy. My clingy dress crept up my thighs, but I knew what I was doing, giving him a show. I felt a heady rush that caused me to strut even more while I smoothed my hands down my sides. I wanted to torment him and make him long for me. For the first time I understood the power I possessed as I watched Nando relax against the doorjamb, his gaze careless, not looking for silhouettes slinking through the shadows but transfixed on me.

When I stood in front of him, he touched my lips, the taste of nicotine on his fingers. His hand trailed over my chin to my neck, my skin bristling where he touched me, the intimacy unbearable, though I didn't let my smile falter.

"Go slower," I whispered, gently pushing him away to make him a clear target for Trek, who crept up behind him. "I don't even know your name," I lied again.

"Come inside and I'll tell you." Nando smiled sweetly and, as he reached for my hand, Trek lunged from the dark and slammed a brick into his face.

Nando reeled into his apartment, spitting teeth, his eyes savage, wide open and searching for a weapon.

"*Puta* bitch!" he screamed, before the brick came down on his shoulder and he fell against the coffee table. A wooden bowl toppled, spilling oranges, which bounced over and around him. His fingers scrabbled across the linoleum, reaching in front of him, as he squirmed toward the TV, where a nine-millimeter pistol lay on the floor.

Trek dropped the brick, stepped back to me, took the gun from my hand and, switching off the safety, walked into the room, his heavy shoes kicking the oranges aside. He stomped on Nando's wrist and aimed the gun at his head. "You've been avoiding me," he said. "And we had a deal. We need to talk."

I bolted down the hallway, not used to running in heels. My ankles wobbled and I stumbled. I kicked off the spiky shoes, left them, and ran barefoot, the wet carpet squishing between my toes.

Outside, I leaned against the Mercedes and stared despondently at the children still playing on the school grounds. I wondered if my mother had despised the men who had brought her gifts. Maybe she had taken drugs to escape the revulsion she'd felt when they'd touched her. For the first time, I felt sorry for her, not angry. Her easy life had had an ugly price.

The *beep* of the car unlocking surprised me. I never heard the gunshot. Had there been one? Trek stepped toward me with lazy ease, his dark eyes catching the light from the setting sun. Except for the blood on his hands, he looked like someone who might be on his way to work.

Magnolia petals dropped from the trees and hit the car hood as he used the tail of his shirt to wipe the blood and tears from my face, his gaze somber. He didn't speak until we were driving past Tulley's liquor store.

"Why did you run?" He sounded angry. "I wouldn't have let Nando hurt you."

"I thought you were going to shoot him."

"*You* were going to shoot him." Trek laughed, his sullen mood broken. "What's the difference who fires?"

I shrugged.

"I only used the gun to make sure he listened to me," Trek explained. "How did you disarm him, anyway?"

"He shot at the kids who were on the steps. I didn't even think. I was just so mad, I grabbed the gun."

Trek stopped the car in front of my grandmother's house. The roses, bending in the evening breeze, spilled petals over the grass.

"You're incredible," Trek said, leaning closer. "Beautiful and fierce." His lips touched mine, soft and warm, and tasting of mint, and as his hands smoothed around my waist, I pulled away, my breath shallow, my mind disoriented from the clashing emotions of hate and anger and desire. My traitor body enjoyed the tenderness in his touch and wanted more.

"How can you?" I said. "Melissa—"

"—means nothing to me," he cut in before I could finish.

"You let her do the rollins!" I grabbed my purse and opened the car door. "You told her . . . you made her believe you loved her. You're everything to her and you did that?"

"Is it my fault if she loves me so much? I thought she'd forget about me by now," he said.

I scrambled out of the car and looked back at him, hating him for deceiving Melissa. "That kiss won't ever happen again."

"Are you challenging me?" he asked as the last bit of sunlight faded into gray.

"I'm warning you." I pulled my hammer from my purse.

"I love girls who play hard to get, and you're the hardest I've ever met. This game won't end until you're dead in love with me. I promise you that."

I slammed the door and, as the car pulled away from the curb, I brought the hammer down and smashed the taillight, the red plastic cover shattered, the bulb inside burst. I gripped the steel handle and braced my bare feet in the grass, expecting Trek to stop the car and charge back at me.

He kept driving. His gleeful smile in the rearview mirror

enraged me. I hurled the hammer and watched it fly, end over end, and thump off the back fender, barely making a dent.

As I walked down the street to retrieve the hammer, a tremor of premonition came over me that my future and Trek's were on an inescapable collision course.

18

I drifted up from sleep, not wanting to leave the dream, where I was safe on a craggy desert plateau with my father. But a strong, intuitive sense of danger kept pulling me away from the arid landscape until, wary and alert, I opened my eyes to the night shadows that swooped across the living room. I was surprised to find myself on the couch. I had only intended to rest there for a moment.

Wind shrilled against the house and, in its lull, hushed voices came from behind the front door. Quick, impatient knocks hit the wood. Immediately, footsteps clanked down the porch steps. Maybe Nando had recognized me, after all, and he and his home-boys were waiting for me on the front lawn, their black trench coats flapping in the turbulence.

I rolled off the couch, the plastic slipcover crackling beneath me, and fell on the rug, my fingers sliding through the velvety fibers as I crawled to the window. Tree shadows, in disarray from the gusts, whirled back and forth over beer cans and puffed-out grocery bags that tumbled down the street, but no posse of Lobos stood in the yard.

I pressed my cheek against the cool glass and still saw no one. Just when I had convinced myself that the sounds had only been trailing fragments from my dream, two faces popped up in front of the window. I startled back, catching my scream, as I recognized Satch and Rico.

"Not funny," I scolded before my relief burst into laughter. I rushed to the door and swung it open.

Dressed in shirts and ties, Satch and Rico met me on the bottom step, their shirttails loose and rippling in the wind. Rico lost his smile and gripped the handrail, then my arm. "Who'd you get vamped up for?"

"Are you going out with someone?" Satch asked at the same time.

I'd forgotten that I was still wearing the clothes that I'd used to lure Nando. "Melissa made me over," I said. "Do you like my new look?"

"I liked the way you looked before, but if you did this for me, then I love it." Rico squeezed me against him, his lips nuzzling my ear, his hands trailing down my back. I pulled away from his kiss and glanced at Satch, who stared out at the street, the grocery flyers skimming over the pavement, apparently more interesting than my half-naked body.

"We've come to say we're sorry," Rico said. "But that doesn't mean we're okay with you being Trek's lure."

I was never going to tell them about Nando. "Why are you

two dressed like church boys?" I asked, steering the conversation away from me.

"We're going to a dance and want you to come with us." Satch held up three red tickets and gave me a glance in which his eyes scanned down, up, and away.

"How 'bout it?" Rico said. "No other gangsters, no guns, just regular kids having fun. Want to be a nobody for a night?"

"As long as you can guarantee it's only for one night." I laughed.

"We change back into gangsters at midnight." Satch grinned. "I promise."

After pulling on black leggings and my gray school sweater, I slipped into my shoes and joined Satch and Rico, the scent of the approaching storm sweeping around us.

Happiness was still building inside me as we walked past the squad cars parked in front of the community center. The officers ignored the thudding background music that shimmied their cars, their focus on the teens who looked ready to break into mob rule. Gathered at the curb, the energy coming off them was sharper than the wind. The guys glowered, cigarettes pinched as they smoked to the filters, but when they saw Rico and Satch, they moseyed across the street to get away from the real gangsters. The laughter from the few girls, Kaylee among them, pierced the music, their frozen-on smiles not hiding the desperation in their eyes.

I started to wave, wishing Kaylee and I could be friends again, but she turned away and stole a cigarette from one of the guys, drew in deeply as she pressed herself against him, then spun back around and blew smoke at me.

"Ignore her," Rico said, pulling me inside.

After stepping through the metal detector, Satch handed our tickets to a woman with gray hair whose orange acrylic nails were as long as knives. She stepped aside and we entered the dimly lit auditorium.

On a raised platform in the far corner, a girl from school stood with the DJ and censored the songs to ensure the lyrics didn't offend the women in the chief of police's granny corps, who had organized the dance as part of their ongoing war against gangs.

Handmade signs on the walls read: *No porn dancing allowed. No Freaking. No Grinding. No Doggy-Dancing. No Front-Piggy-Backing. No Hiking Up Skirts. No Hands-On-the-Floor Dancing.* To enforce the rules, chaperones patrolled the dance floor armed with flashlights. The beams swirled over the dancers, spotlighting couples who danced too close or too *nasty*.

"Are you going to stay after reading the rules?" Dante bumped against me, looking sozzled, his eyes red and unfocused. "Everyone knows you like to dance crazy."

"Get lost." I shoved him away, surprised to see him here.

He leaned closer, his breath spiking the air between us with the sweet scent of alcohol. He held up a plastic water bottle, the liquid inside clear, though I doubted it was water. "Take this as my peace offering. Instant drunk. No kidding."

Rico appeared from behind me and snatched the bottle from Dante. "What are you giving her?"

134

"My grandpa's white lightning," Dante said proudly. "It's his home brew. He's got a still in the basement."

"That better be true." Rico twisted off the cap, took one sip, then guzzled half the liquid. "Whoa." His face pinched. "It's rocket fuel." He handed the bottle to Satch, who took a long swallow.

"The buzz is instantaneous." Satch pretended to stagger before he passed the bottle to me.

The alcohol overwhelmed my taste buds, then stung my throat as it burned down and curled into my stomach. "It's going to set me on fire," I choked.

Dante took the bottle and drained it, his eyes watering from the burn. "The fire's what makes it so good."

"Do you have any to sell?" Rico asked.

"I got a crate of merchandise around the corner, outside, but for friends it's free." Dante stumbled toward the exit. "Come on."

Rico turned to me. "Save your kisses for me, Blaise," he teased, gently punching my chin before he hurried after Dante as the music changed to a love song, the rhythm slow and sultry.

I wanted to dance, but Satch looked ready to desert me for the girl who was sending him flirty smiles. *Too bad for her.* The liquor had emboldened me and I smoothed my hands around him, trapping him as he started to leave.

His breath caught, as if I had stung him. I thought he was going to push me away. Instead, his hands slid to my waist and he pressed me gently against him. A pleasant shock rushed through me.

"You're trembling," I said, racing my palms up his back, absorbing the heat of his body.

"So are you," he whispered and, as he found the music's rhythm, I felt the sensual movement of his muscles beneath my fingertips.

The beam from a flashlight spun over my face, circling like an agitated fly. I didn't want to release Satch, but the chaperone kept me under the light until I loosened my grip.

We eased apart and stood motionless, gazing at each other even after the music changed to a rapid beat and all around us dancers swiveled and pumped.

"What are you doing?" Rico yelled, suddenly returning to the dance floor, seeming unaware of how closely I had danced with Satch. Or maybe he was too drunk to care. His eyes watered as if he had chugged a bottle of booze before coming back inside. He attacked the music, his arms wild, more bottles in his pockets and waistband, protruding beneath his shirt. "Move! Why are you just standing there staring at each other?"

For the rest of the night, I danced between Satch and Rico, gliding against one and then the other, but not with my usual moves. I didn't want the flashlights to spotlight me.

Even so, the girls who stood against the wall, the ones I saw crying in the school bathrooms, watched me, their eyes hard and resentful that I danced with two guys while they danced with none. They spoke behind their hands to hide their lips. I could just imagine what they were saying about me.

"The old rumors about you being with me and Satch at the same time are going to spread around school again," Rico teased.

I shrugged. I was still a virgin, though the girls glaring at me were not. It wasn't desire for the boys that made them sleep around as much as baby hunger. They wanted a baby to fill their loneliness.

At the end of the dance, Satch, Rico, and I joined the crowd sweeping outside, into the storm, where a line of cars waited on the street. Everyone had rides home, except for us. We were the strays who strolled down the alley, sloshing through puddles, the night shuddering with supernatural light. Even the spider webs glistened, misty with rain.

I slowed my pace when a car turned the corner, headlights askew, one lantern pushed sideways on a dented fender. The driver had turned off the windshield wipers, and raindrops glimmered golden on the glass, hiding whoever sat behind the steering wheel.

Rico seemed unconcerned about the car rolling toward us. The alcohol had killed his normal vigilance.

"Do you recognize the bucket?" I asked.

"I'd remember an old wreck like that one," Satch said. "Maybe it's someone's new ride to work."

The car hitched forward, the window came down, and Trek leaned out, the rain drumming his face. "Jump in," he urged. "You're getting wet."

"We can't get any wetter than we are," I said, certain Trek had been driving around searching for me. At the same time, I had a terrible feeling that running into Dante hadn't been an accident either.

"Where are you off to?" Rico asked, too drunk to feel suspicious, when normally he would never have trusted this kind of coincidence, especially one that involved Trek.

"I'm going down to the Tidal Basin to catch some lightning," Trek replied. "Want to go?"

A chill came over me. "Why did you have to steal a car for that?"

"The forecast calls for hail," he said too quickly. "Do you think I want to put dings in my car when a dozen more dents in this one won't make any difference?"

I had no answer, though my wariness intensified. I couldn't imagine Trek paying attention to the weather.

Satch gazed up at the clouds aflutter with sheet lightning. "Let's do it."

"You're too drunk," I warned.

I had played the game in seventh grade with Rico during a storm like this one. We had gripped the railing that encircled the Tidal Basin and waited, rain pelting us as thunderbolts crackled across the dark sky. Even after static had raced over my skin and lifted my hair in tendrils above my head, the thrill, the utter exhilaration, had kept my hands clasped to the metal. When Rico let go, I had wrenched free, diving into the wet grass where we rolled together, losing the charge, victorious over the lightning that had hit the railing and thrown jagged spikes into the cherry trees.

Rico had said, "It's the adrenaline. Isn't it the best feeling in the world?"

It was.

The sound of the car door opening pulled me back from the memory.

"We won't make you watch," Rico said. "We'll drop you off at your house. Get in."

"I'm going with you," I argued, throwing myself onto the backseat, which smelled of wet feathers and dog hair. "Someone will have to identify your charred bodies."

Rico slammed the door and squeezed in front next to Satch, who had opened another bottle of booze.

Thunder crashed, the vibration shuddering through the car, as we started forward.

A few blocks later, Trek drove onto the lot of a convenience store. "I should have checked the gas gauge before I stole the car," he announced. "We're running on fumes. I need to fill up the tank."

"Then why did you drive past the pumps?" I asked.

"I want some brew, is that okay?" Trek said as he continued around to the Dumpsters in back.

"Of course," I muttered.

Drenched and shivering, I decided to leave them, buy a coffee, and walk home. Satch and Rico no longer needed me to watch over them. They were going to be too knocked-out drunk to hold on to the railing, anyway. I climbed out of the car before Trek turned off the engine.

"Blaise, stay here," Trek called after me.

The very tone of his voice should have warned me to go back, but I tramped through the puddles to the front of the store and pushed inside.

The smells of coffee and grilling hot dogs hit me on a wave of heat as a loud *buzz* announced my arrival. The cashier didn't bother to glance up from the magazine she was reading. She kept her face down, but even so I caught a glimpse of silver rings that pierced her eyebrows, lips, and nose. The face metal presented a tough image, as did her jet black, dyed hair, cut short and choppy. The only thing girlie about her were the stars inked into bracelets on her pale wrists. I smiled to myself, knowing she wouldn't need to dress so dangerous if she really was.

I rounded the counter and bumped into the boy who had let me into Nando's apartment. He looked up, startled, his coat pockets bulging with chocolate bars, the bottoms of his pajamas dripping rainwater. He had apparently snuck out of his home, barefooted, to come here and steal candy.

"You're a pitiful thief," I said in a low voice. "Do you want to break your mama's heart?"

He shook his head but he didn't put the candy back, either. His gaze shifted to the cashier, who was still reading, her face hidden. Maybe all the kids who lived nearby snuck out of bed to rob the store on her shift.

I handed him a twenty, the bill wet from my rain-soaked pocket. "Use this to buy the chocolate so you don't end up at the police station tonight. Your mom probably needs her sleep."

He gave me a sweet smile. "Can I keep the change?"

"What for?"

"My sister's birthday," he said earnestly.

I rolled my eyes, then smiled. "You can have what's left after you buy my coffee." I stepped around him, not understanding why I suddenly needed to set a good example.

As I grabbed a paper cup, I became aware of someone moving in the liquor aisle behind me. Less than twenty feet away Nando stood in front of the refrigeration unit that held the beer.

Scabs encrusted his lips, his face swollen over knobby bruises. Under his right eye, the black threads hanging off the irregular stitches gave me the impression that he had sewn the skin together himself with a needle and thread taken from someone's sewing kit.

He popped the tab on a beer and drank it where he stood. When he set the empty on the refrigerator shelf, he must have caught my reflection in the glass, because he turned without warning and lunged at me.

I could feel his hatred and took a quick step backward, searching for a weapon, when the deafening blasts of gunfire stopped me. Trek held an AK-47 assault rifle, his eyes fiery with excitement. He had removed the flash suppressor and, when he fired, a long white flame streamed from the muzzle. Bullets riddled the wall above me, crossing the convex mirror that shielded the surveillance camera. Glass burst apart and, glittering, spiraled down, the shards falling on Nando, who pulled a gun from his waistband as he dived behind a wine display. Bottles exploded and the fruity scent of grapes splattered around me.

The boy! I could feel his panic before I found his gaze. He stared at me, shivering violently, his hands over his ears against the thunder of the firing guns. Not knowing where to run and with no place to hide, he had crouched on the floor, an easy target. I raced to him, my heart jolting, adrenaline throbbing through my veins, while brass bullet casings hopped and pinged across the floor and snapped against my legs.

Before I could reach him, bullets tore through his jacket. He screamed, calling for his mother, as plumes of crimson puffed from his chest. Breathing in the blood-misted air, I fell beside him and pulled him into my arms. The shooting stopped and, through the echo of gunfire, I heard a cry gurgle from the boy's throat.

I cradled his small torn body, the scents of chocolate and blood and wine blending into the fetid odors brought from death. My lungs strained to find oxygen in the smoke and blood-thick air.

Rico and Satch crashed through the door. Specks of the boy's shredded coat floated around them as they joined me, their faces hardening to hide their sorrow while Trek strode toward us, triumphant.

"Did I, or did I not, promise to kill Nando if he touched you? And he touched you, didn't he? So it's his own damn fault he's dead, isn't it?"

I forced my lips into a grim smile and rose as I calculated my chances of disarming Trek before he could fire and kill me.

Rico yanked me against him and, half-dragging me, took me outside into the downpour, his tender, tough grip strangling my fight. "It's suicide what you're thinking," he said against my ear. "We can't do anything while Trek is the only one with a gun."

Laughing, Trek followed us outside, Satch close behind him. "This will make the nightly news!" Trek yelled, face up to the storm. "Civilians are going to be afraid to stop at a convenience store. Because of me! I'm nothing but terror, roaming the night, policing with my own justice."

Trek thrust the assault rifle in front of me. The barrel hissed and steamed in the rain, the vapor warm on my face. I had heard the ritual described enough times to know what happened next.

I had to place my fingerprints on the weapon in a show of solidarity to affirm my silence.

Satch grabbed hold, as did Rico.

At last, I clutched the barrel, the metal scalding my skin.

The ritual complete, we returned to the car as sirens broke through the unrelenting sound of rain.

19

The windshield wipers screeched back and forth, but we could still hear the wail of sirens coming at us from every direction. I fought back tears and watched Trek's reflection in the rearview mirror, the thrill in his eyes, his creepy grin. He was enjoying this.

"When I stop, we dump the car and run in different directions," Trek said, his breath coming hard and fast.

"We know the drill." Rico sounded totally sober at this point.

I inhaled too deeply. The air caught in my throat and came out, a thin sigh. Rico squeezed my elbow and, from the front seat, Satch shot me a warning glance. Trek would see any show of sadness as criticism for what he had done, and he was still the only one with a gun.

In the distance, police lights pulsed, growing brighter. The siren shrilled, rising and falling, then rising again.

I stared at the sky. My grandmother would never recover once she found out that I had been involved in a double murder. The killing of a child. I imagined her devastation as Trek took a hard right, pushing the speed limit.

The car swerved around the corner, my insides sliding with it. Tires shrieked into a skid and the nauseating smell of burnt rubber seeped into the car. My stomach rippled, creeping up, the nausea too strong to quell. Saliva flooded my mouth. I leaned over and vomited behind Trek's seat.

Coughing and spitting, I remained with my head between my knees until Rico pulled me up, unbuttoned his shirt and used his wet shirttail to wipe my face. I leaned against him and gazed out the window, my mind blank, color fading from my vision.

Trek caught my stare in the rearview mirror. "Blaise is going into shock."

Satch looked back at me. "She'll never be able to run when we ditch the car."

"One of you take her home and get her warm." Trek slammed on the brakes, a panic stop. Uncontrolled, the car spun out and continued to slide into the curb. Hubcaps scraped against the concrete, bluish-white sparks spraying as high as the window.

The moment the car came to rest under the low-hanging branches of a tree, Satch leaped out and wrenched open the back door. Together, he and Rico pulled me into the blustering wind.

The rain had stopped. Moon-silvered clouds swept across the sky, trailing the storm, and from all around us came the sound of dripping water.

Satch felt my forehead, his hand sliding down to my cheek. "She's stone cold and not even shivering."

"Stop talking," Trek yelled, the engine revving.

"I'll stay with Trek," Satch said.

"Decide!" Trek shouted, the car nosing forward.

Abruptly, Rico jumped into the front seat, the decision made. The car rocketed down the street, Satch staring after it as if he couldn't believe he had been left to take care of me.

In the opposite direction three blocks away, a squad car shot around the corner, bar lights flashing. I stood unmoving beneath the trees, aware of the headlights reflecting in white smears on the wet pavement.

Before the police were close enough to see me, Satch scooped me into his arms and carried me to a cardboard shelter that a homeless person had abandoned. He nudged a rusted shopping cart away from the entrance and hid me inside under a yellow plastic tarp, the waterlogged cardboard floor squishing beneath me.

He didn't have time to hide himself. The lights from the police car were already flickering over his face. Grabbing the shopping cart like a homeless resident of the Borderlands, he hunched over the handlebar and rolled the cart down the sidewalk in clear view.

The squad car blew straight past him.

When the street became empty again, Satch ran back to me, heaved me into his arms, and jogged away. I glanced up as the night tilted, spinning the stars. And with a sigh, I let go.

Fingers tapped my cheek. I opened my eyes, the air warm and smelling of soap. Satch looked down at me, worry in his frown, his arms holding me upright. "Blaise?"

My toes curled into the fluffy fibers of a bath mat. He had taken off my muddy shoes and carried me inside his house and up the stairs to his bathroom.

"Can you get yourself undressed and into the shower?" He

turned me toward the mirror so I could see my bloodstained clothes. "You need to get cleaned up and warm."

But I had traveled too deep inside myself, and the thought of Satch seeing me naked wasn't enough to make me rise up again.

"Please help me, Blaise. I really don't want to do this." The distress in his voice pulled me to the threshold. I wanted to comfort him, but a stronger force took control and sucked me back into nothingness.

"Okay," he whispered. "I hope you remember this wasn't my choice."

He peeled off my sweater and the sodden dress, after which he unhooked my bra. Looking everywhere but at me, he pulled off my leggings and panties.

When my clothes lay in a heap on the floor, Satch yanked back the plastic shower curtain, the hooks jittering down the rod. Gently, he lifted me and set me standing in the tub. I stared at the showerhead, scaled with mineral deposits, and watched the water sprinkle out.

After testing the temperature, Satch eased me forward and pressed my head under the warm spray. He massaged his aunt's lilac-scented shampoo into my tangled hair. Pink suds slid off my body and foamed around the drain.

When the water became clear, Satch shut off the shower and wrapped a towel around my head. From the hook on the back of the door, he grabbed his aunt's robe and slipped my arms into the sleeves. The thin material adhered to my skin, soaking up the water that Satch had been too timid to pat dry with a towel.

He carried me to his room, set me on his bed, and tucked the covers around me, his scent laced in their warmth. I felt his lips against my forehead, probably to gauge my temperature, as my grandmother used to do when I was a child.

"Oh, Blaise," he murmured.

From the agony in his voice, I assumed my fever was high.

When he finally pulled away, he patted my shoulder. "Try to sleep."

The moment I dozed off, the nightmare came, vivid and immediate. The boy was stealing candy, unmindful of the danger. Within the eerie logic of the dream, I believed that if I could reach him before Trek shot him, then I could pull him back into life with me. I raced to the boy as bullets shredded his heart, his blood splattering over me.

I startled awake, fighting the hands that held me, until I realized Satch was lifting me against the pillows.

He had changed into dry clothes, his hair wet and combed as if he had taken a shower. "You need something in your stomach." He held the warm rim of a cup against my lips. "Sip this. You'll feel better with something inside you."

Creamy hot cocoa melted over my tongue, the scent of chocolate steaming across my face. My stomach contracted and I burst from my daze. "He was just a kid stealing candy. He shouldn't be dead."

"He was eleven." Rico's sudden appearance in the doorway silenced me. His face relaxed when he saw that I seemed responsive. "Blaise," he began gently. "Nando wasn't just a Lobo in the wrong place at the wrong time. Trek was killing him *for you*."

I winced as a cold shudder raced through my body.

"Tell us what happened," Satch said softly.

My tears began to fall as I described luring Nando, leaving out the parts that I thought might anger Rico.

He and Satch listened sympathetically, seeming to understand too well that sometimes the wrong choice felt like the right one.

When I finished, Rico said, "Trek was so eager to impress you that he got careless."

"He left a witness," Satch said. "The cashier. I never saw anyone, but I knew someone had to be watching the store."

"I didn't see anyone, either." Rico nodded. "After Trek and I ditched the car, I went back and stood with the gawkers behind the crime scene tape. I heard someone say that the cashier never got a look at the killer's face."

"That won't matter to Trek," Satch said bitterly. "He's like my dad. He always kills the witnesses. That's why he took out the boy."

"What about us?" I asked. "We're witnesses."

Rico turned my hand to show me the raw blisters where I'd grabbed the gun. "You're safe. You swore your loyalty when you put your fingerprints on the weapon."

I nodded, but the sinking feeling inside me didn't go away.

Still holding my hand, Rico said, "You haven't told us everything, Blaise. Trek said that he had promised to kill Nando if he touched you. And Nando touched you, but you didn't tell us about that."

"She told us enough," Satch said quickly. "We don't need to hear her describe that."

Rico ignored Satch, anger firing his eyes, and I knew this was personal, between him and me. Moving closer, his teeth gritted, Rico said, "I want to hear how you pushed Nando away. Did you tell him you weren't ready?"

I stiffened.

"Come off it, Rico," Satch burst in. "She couldn't. She was setting him up."

Rico glared at me. "You let him touch you, didn't you?"

When I didn't answer, Rico dodged into Satch's closet and came back out, snapping a clip into a gun.

"Man," Satch groaned. "Haven't we had enough for one night?"

"I owe the Lobos a payback," Rico said with an edge to his voice. "Tonight's perfect. All their homeboys will be here and in Mass 5, trying to track down Nando's killer." He dodged into the hallway. "And when they get home, they'll find any cars they left behind riddled with bullets."

I fell back on my pillow, imagining children diving under their beds from fear.

"This is my fault," I said.

"No," Satch whispered. "Rico knows it's his fault. That's why he's so damn angry. If he'd stood up to Trek and stopped him, this whole thing with Nando would never have happened." Satch pulled the covers over me. "Try to get some sleep, now."

But I couldn't. All I could think about was how Trek always killed his witnesses.

20

I filled the teakettle with water, set it on the stove, and stared at the flame, trying to plan the next week. For eight days, I had evaded Trek. I intended to never lure for him again and had returned to dressing tough and tomboy. But with that decision, I had lost my source of income; my only way to help my grandmother. This morning, she had come home from work half-dead, and hadn't even changed out of her work clothes before collapsing across her bed. I had taken off her shoes and rubbed her back while she drifted into sleep. The deepness of her slumber had frightened me.

Overhead the drone of her fan buzzed through the ceiling and into the kitchen, vibrating the walls, a relentless reminder that I had to find a way to make money. I considered shoplifting, becoming what people in the neighborhood called "a person who can get things." I thought about selling drugs, but I'd seen their effects on my mother and on too many kids at my school, and I couldn't bring myself to do that.

The teakettle shrilled, jarring me from my thoughts. I poured water over the tea bag, steam rising warm against my face. Then, suddenly, a prickling of gooseflesh raced up my arms. I saw the boy at the kitchen table, his gaze solemn, filling me with guilt. I ran my fingers over my neck, trying to calm the blood racing to my head before he disappeared with a whiff of cool air that drifted over me.

I set the cup down, swung my purse strap over my shoulder, and left for school. I didn't need the district's grief counselor to explain to me that because I couldn't allow my grief full expression, it had festered in the unconscious layers of my mind and was making me see things that weren't there.

Near school, I paused, surprised to see Kaylee and Melissa standing together. Kaylee looked as if she hadn't gotten any sleep the night before, dark slashes under her eyes, her hair uncombed and knotted in a spiky mess on top of her head, while Melissa appeared to have spent an hour in front of a mirror perfecting her makeup and curling her glossy hair.

They were frowning at each other, arguing about something. I strolled closer, hoping to pick up a few words.

"You're such a liar," Melissa said, her scowl deepening as she bit at the side of her fingernail. "Why do you keep telling me such horrible things about Trek?"

"Why would I make up something like that?" Kaylee shot back.

"Because you're jealous and want to ruin it for me." Melissa shoved Kaylee against a car and stomped away.

"You're going to wish you had listened to me," Kaylee shouted.

"Just leave me alone," Melissa pleaded.

When I realized she was crying, I started after her, but Rico and Satch cut me off, their grim expressions stopping me.

"What's up?" I asked, a feeling of dread rising inside me.

"A reward's been offered to anyone who can provide information about the killing of the boy." Satch handed me a flyer.

My chest ached when I looked down at the picture of the boy's smiling face. "Fifty thousand dollars," I whispered. "Does Trek know?"

"We haven't been hanging out at his house," Rico said. "But when he sees this, he's going to go ballistic."

As they left me, I wondered how high the reward had to go before Trek worried that we might snitch. Fifty grand was a temptation. I thought about the difference that much money could make in my life and, without warning, an image of Gabriella burst into my mind. What would my life today be like if she had lived?

Angrily, I pushed the thought aside and entered the school. I didn't have time to think about something that could never be.

In the hallway, Ariel joined me, smiling. "Guess what?" she said excitedly.

I loved the happiness I saw in her eyes. "Tell me."

"I'm going to California!" She pulled a printout map of Venice Beach from her canvas tote. "Can you believe it?"

"When?" I asked, a mix of emotions rushing through me.

"This summer. I can't wait."

"Are you moving?" I said, feeling suddenly left behind.

"Danny and I are going."

I sucked in air and looked around to make sure no one had heard her. I couldn't hide my distress. I couldn't even force a smile.

Her head dropped, and when she lifted it again, her smile was gone. "Can't you be happy for me, Blaise?"

"Ariel, how are you going to do this? You don't have the money."

"A bus ticket doesn't cost that much, and we're saving money from his sales." She shrugged, smiling dreamily. "It's not like we don't know how to get by on nothing. We'll manage. We're going to finish school there, together."

"I'm scared for you, Ariel. You got to . . ." My voice broke and I realized I was crying.

Easing closer, she stroked my hair. "He's not like those thugs that I've been with before," she said in a hushed voice. "I can have a future with him. He's decent."

"A drug dealer?"

"That's the reason he wants to move," Ariel said sincerely. "He hates what he does."

I wiped at my tears. "Please check it out more before you go."

"That's all I've been doing."

I nodded but still wasn't convinced.

"Don't be so sad," she said. "You'll come visit us. I've planned that, too. Start saving for a bathing suit." She gave me a quick hug before she dashed into her classroom.

For a second, I stood in the empty hallway, taken in by what she'd said. I imagined myself walking on a long stretch of beach, breathing the ocean air. No fear, no worries, only the crash of waves and seagulls swooping around me—but then I remembered where we lived, and a desperate cry escaped me.

At the end of the school day, I was still worrying about Ariel, afraid that her excitement was making her careless. I crossed the teachers' parking lot, not watching where I was going, and a history textbook flew past me, inches from hitting my shoulder. I spun around as the edge of the spine slammed into Dante, who stood less than three feet behind me. The binding snapped and pages tumbled across the pavement, catching on the legs of students who were talking in small groups.

I turned back to see who had thrown the book and gaped at Kaylee, who looked close to tears.

"Don't you ever touch me again!" she screamed at Dante.

"Or what?" He snickered. A long scratch bled down his neck. "You took the back stairwell. I figured you were looking for me."

In response, Kaylee threw her geometry book at him. The text thumped against his chest and fell on top of the history book with a loud *thwack*.

Smirking, Dante lit a cigarette as I eased closer. He tossed the match, and blew the smoke out at Kaylee. His excitement sickened me. I dropped my purse, snatched the cigarette from him, and ground it out on the back of his hand. He screamed and jerked back, the air filling with the stench of scorched skin. Cursing me, he flicked his fingers to get rid of the ember, then examined the burn before he looked at me and drew his hand back in a fist, expecting me to flinch.

"Come on." I stared defiantly at him, waiting for his punch.

I wanted to fight. Pain. Bruises. Blood. That kind of hurt was easy compared to what I was holding inside me.

"I've had a bad week," I said, stretching my arms out to my sides. "And I'd like nothing more than to bloody your face and beat you into the ground. I'll give you the first shot, but I'll win anyway."

"Like hell," he shouted for the few students who had gathered to watch, but the fear that I might humiliate him again in front of our classmates had weakened his resolve. He'd already lost too much respect because of me, and I could feel him backing away from a confrontation.

"You're not worth my time." He veered off, lighting another cigarette, and ambled across the parking lot to join his wannabe friends, who were pretending they hadn't seen our face-off.

I stepped over to Kaylee, who was picking up her books, and helped her gather the pages that had blown free.

"What happened?" I asked as we stood.

"My mom was hospitalized last night." She drew in a ragged breath, her hands trembling. "I needed to get home to take care of my sisters, so I wasn't as careful as I usually am. I knew better. I shouldn't have taken the back stairs. Security guards are never there this time of day, but Dante was, and he grabbed me."

"We should report him," I said, looking around for the security guards.

"Reporting it just makes it worse," Kaylee said. "You know that. No one cares."

A sudden shift in the noise drew my attention to the kids who had been standing in small groups on the lot. Their laughter had stopped. No one was talking. They were easing away, slipping behind the teachers' cars.

"Do you see anyone with a gun?" I asked.

Before Kaylee could answer, the scent of Trek's aftershave breezed over me. I gripped her arm and, turning slowly, weighed our chances of leaving before Trek saw us.

He was staring straight at me, smiling at my expression, his white T-shirt not large enough to hide the outline of the gun holstered in his waistband.

Kaylee hissed and, before I could stop her, she dropped her books, slammed in front of me, and spit on Trek. "I hate you," she shouted.

Her outburst terrified me. "No, Kaylee!" I tried to pull her back.

Trek wiped the saliva off his arm and smeared it across her lips.

She slugged him, her hands slapping blindly until he caught her wrists and bent her arms behind her. Holding her hands pinned against her back, he forced her to rest her head against his chest.

"You didn't win," she said bitterly.

"Was it a competition?" he asked. "Is that what you think it was?"

Tears welled into her eyes.

I stared at Kaylee, sickened, suddenly knowing whose name she wrote on the soles of her shoes. My heart pounded, a battering ram of emotions. "Let her go."

Trek smiled at me and pressed her tighter against him. "What do you think you're going to do about it?"

"You won't back down, but neither will I."

He laughed. "You want to fight me?"

When I didn't answer, his eyes became tense, radiating danger. "Do you think I'm Dante?" he asked softly.

I could feel the tension vibrating between us but said nothing and stood my ground. If it came to a showdown, I'd be left bloodied on the pavement.

To my relief, Trek smiled and loosened his hold on Kaylee. His hands smoothed up her arms to her shoulders, then to her neck, where his fingers lingered, his touch tender.

Tears rolled down her cheeks when he held her face and forced her to look at him. "I don't need to fight you anymore, do I, Kaylee?"

"Why bother?" she said sadly. "You already took everything you wanted from me."

Trek let her go. Without looking at me, she picked up her books, ignoring the pages that had scattered across the pavement, and walked away, her posture showing her defeat. She still loved him.

I rushed after her. "Kaylee!"

Trek grabbed my arm and pulled me back with such force, I fell against him.

"Do you think I came here to have it out with Kaylee?" he asked. "You're the one I've been looking for. What's up?"

I said nothing.

"Are Satch and Rico the reason you've been keeping yourself from me?" he asked.

"No," I said sharply.

"I should have shredded them the night I got rid of Nando. They're making me into a fool. I gave them a lure and they still haven't gotten Danny."

"It's my fault." The words rushed out when I saw Satch and Rico striding across the parking lot toward us. "I've been busy with school and my grandmother—"

"I can see through your lies," Trek warned. "And I like the challenge of figuring out what's really going on in your mind. Maybe I'll find something that you've even hidden from yourself."

I sighed. "It's been hard. What do you think? The boy is dead."

"That doesn't mean a thing," he said angrily. "You better learn that fast and get used to the killing."

"I don't want to, ever."

"You got to, Blaise," he said, softening his tone. His hand rubbed my shoulder. "We don't have a choice. Death lives here, with us."

"Who lives here?" Rico joined us, his eyes on Trek, who ignored him.

Satch stood like a mountain beside me.

"Get Danny tonight," Trek ordered. "He'll be at his usual spot near Tulley's selling to my customers."

"Why tonight?" Satch asked.

"Just do it." Trek left us standing in the emptied parking lot, the pages from Kaylee's history book twirling around us.

"I got a bad feeling about this," Satch said as soon as Trek was out of hearing range. "We should wait."

"Something's wrong," Rico agreed.

From behind them, standing where only I could see him, Trek pulled the gun from his waistband and aimed, first at Rico, and then at Satch. Grinning at me, he slipped the weapon back under his T-shirt and continued across the lot, leaving me paralyzed with fear.

I grasped my throat, trying to breathe, and said in a thin voice. "I'll lure Danny."

"You promised you'd never do that again," Rico said. "Why the sudden change?"

"Do you always need to have an explanation?" I said with an explosion of anger that silenced him. My entire body was shaking. "Maybe if we bust Danny's face, Trek will leave us alone."

21

Four hours later I left my house, and after five blocks of walking in platform shoes that blistered my toes, I reached Tulley's. Three men sat on the benches in front, talking sports and sipping orange sodas, the air around them scented with soap from their after-work showers. They fell silent as I strode past them, the tap of my heels the only sound in the nighttime quiet. I could feel them watching me and felt uncomfortable, queasy even, in my skimpy torn skirt that was more advertisement than clothing. I had done my own makeup this time. I wanted Danny to recognize me.

Quickening my pace, I dodged into the alley and didn't slow down until I reached the stone house with the iron fence where Satch and Rico waited, hidden in the ivy, the glossy leaves shimmering from the streetlight. Though neither spoke, I nodded my understanding; I had to bring Danny back to where they stood.

Staying behind the shelter of trees, I stole into the Borderlands, the air suddenly too sour to breathe. The odor came off a girl, my age, who moved in jerks and hitches, her face scaled with scabs. An unlit cigarette, half-eaten and stuck on her bottom lip, bobbed as she counted out dollar bills that looked slimy with dirt.

Though I had seen no one down the street, when she waved the money, Danny rode his bicycle out of the crevice between two row houses and pedaled toward her. Nighttime sales required more caution.

Straddling his bike, he took her money and, in exchange, handed her a deflated red balloon that held her drugs. Impatient to get high again, she scurried away, coughing her lungs clear as she crawled under the porch where she most likely lived.

Danny folded the bills into a Ziploc bag that was fat with money, then tucked it into the waistband of his spotless jeans, and rode away.

I stepped into the street and called after him. "Hey, Danny!"

"Blaise?" Leaning to the left, he guided the bike back to me, the ankh that Ariel had given him reflecting the streetlight.

A sudden breeze swelled my torn skirt, showing off my legs and curves, but Danny never glanced down. From the way he focused on the empty buildings behind me, I knew Ariel had told him what I was doing for Trek.

He braked in front of me. "You look beautiful." He grinned. "You could stop any guy dead in his tracks."

His choice of words spun an icy foreboding down my spine, but I smiled sweetly and, forcing a laugh, said, "That's what I'm supposed to do."

"Did you come here after me?" he asked, kidding around but also serious. "Are Satch and Rico hiding nearby?"

"I'll have to come after you eventually, Danny, but I've already done my job for today," I lied, while playing with the skirt I had torn before leaving home. "I came here after to catch my breath. Sometimes things get too intense, you know?"

He glanced at the rip in the silky material and his grip on the handlebars loosened. "What happened?"

"I don't want to talk about it," I said, staring at his perfect nose, his straight teeth, his sincere eyes that still hadn't looked down at my body. If he would just gawk at my breasts, give me one lascivious glance, then I could do this without remorse, but he didn't. Maybe he was seriously in love with Ariel. My chin started quivering.

Danny bent lower, over the handlebars, so he could see into my eyes. "You look ready to cry. Was it that bad? Did he hurt you?"

"Go away, Danny," I choked. "Just ride away. I need to be alone."

"I'm not going to leave you when you're upset." He swung his leg off his bike, set the kickstand, then took off his white shirt, which smelled of Ariel's perfume, and wrapped it around me. "You're shivering."

"I'm not shivering," I insisted, my emotions unraveling. Was I crying to lure Danny or crying because I *was* luring him? I felt miserable, and that was no act. "Just go. Please."

"It's warm inside Tulley's. I'll buy you a soda and you can tell me what happened." He grabbed the handlebars and began rolling his bike forward, while his left hand guided me toward his ambush.

Because he was worried about me, he had let his guard down and didn't see the shadows racing through the ivy until Satch and Rico sprung out at him.

Terror ripped across Danny's face. He pivoted and tried to mount his bike, but their fists were faster, hammering his arms and cuffing his head, their feet scuffling around his until the bike toppled and Danny fell on top of it.

When he tried to get up, Rico struck his face. Danny turned to escape Rico's blows and Satch nailed him with one punch. His fist slammed into Danny's nose. The cartilage snapped with a sharp *crack* and his blood spattered the gravel.

"Stop!" I screamed.

"We're done." Satch gripped Rico's wrist to keep him from throwing the next punch and held on until Rico's fingers uncurled and his arm went limp, the fight draining from him.

They sprinted away, yelling for me to come with them. I stayed and watched Danny drag himself off the fallen bike. He slumped against a trashcan, blood trickling down his neck and over the silver ankh.

"You bitch," he groaned. "I was trying to help you because you're Ariel's friend." His fingers scrabbled through the weeds, found a rock, and hurled it at me.

It struck my thigh, the pain needle-sharp, his curses hurting me more. I staggered back, despising myself, my arms tightened across my chest, forcing back a wail of despair.

"Blaise, come on!" Rico yelled.

"I'm going to get you, Blaise," Danny said. "I don't care if you are Ariel's friend. You're going to pay for this."

His threat released me from my shame and guilt. "You can try," I whispered. "You can always try."

With deliberate slowness, I took off his shirt, dropped it on his bike, and walked to Rico, who waited for me at the corner.

"Where'd Satch go?" I asked as we raced through the Borderlands.

"Home to get drunk," Rico said.

"Good idea. Let's join him."

We found Satch sitting on his back porch, drinking a beer, two six-packs at his feet.

I kicked off my shoes and slid my blistered toes through the cool grass before collapsing next to him.

"Better drink." Satch handed me a beer as Rico sat beside me, examining the scraped skin on his knuckles.

"I'm going to get blitzed," I announced, snapping the tab. Beer foamed over the top, cold on my fingers, the froth dripping onto my legs. "If I can kill enough brain cells maybe I can forget this night."

I guzzled the first beer and watched the moonrise, remembering a time when something as simple as the night sky had given me a thrill. By the time I had finished my second beer, sirens were rising and falling, their discordant wails causing dogs to howl and yelp.

"Do you think Danny called the cops?" I asked, tossing my empty can into the pile.

Rico shook his head. "He knows the rules. I mean, what did he expect? He was dealing to Trek's regular customers."

I grabbed another beer. "He'll have to go to the hospital," I speculated. "Irwin won't be able to fix his nose. It was smashed back, clear over to the—"

"Shut up about Danny," Satch said. "How are you going to forget if you keep talking about him?"

"It's hard to forget," I said sadly, wondering if Danny had told his homeboys yet. I pictured my grandmother's house punctured with bullet holes, and then I thought of Ariel. Danny had probably called her while he was still on the ground. "Give me another beer," I said gruffly, the wind lifting my skirt.

"We need something to distract ourselves," Rico said, elbowing me playfully. "You dressing like that makes me wonder what you're doing when we're not around. Tell us. Have you lured any guys for yourself?"

"I wouldn't know what to do if I caught one," I said, shrugging his hand off my shoulder.

"Satch and I can help you out," he joked, gripping my knee. "We know what happens next. We'll give you some practice."

I caught his wrist as his fingers smoothed up my thigh. "I'm sure you and Satch don't need any practice."

"We don't, but you do," Rico said.

I felt heat rise to my cheeks and pressed the can of beer against my face.

Rico nudged me. "How many guys have you kissed?"

I stared at the moths, pale in the moonlight, fluttering around the hollyhocks. Did Trek's kiss count? I didn't want his to be my first, though technically, I supposed it was.

"You've never had a real kiss, have you?" Rico teased, his hand settling back on my leg. "You better let me show you how it's done."

I twisted away from him. "Stop it."

"Come on," he said. "You need practice for your first real event."

"You're crazy, Rico," Satch said, crumpling a beer can. "Leave her alone and just let her get drunk."

Instead, Rico stood and pulled me to my feet and into his arms. My beer fell to the concrete and rolled into the grass. I started to push him away but then I saw the sadness in his eyes and felt bad for him.

Behind me, I heard Satch smash another can, but my focus remained on Rico. Maybe it was the beer or my own longing, but I moved my hands up his back, entwining them around his neck. When I felt his body quake, I held him tighter. I knew he was using me to hide his sadness from Satch so he could keep up his hard homeboy front. Though I felt no temptation to do more, I let him kiss me until his need to cry had turned into a need of a different kind.

"You better have another beer," he said softly, looking down at me, his smile slow and lazy, his gaze making me aware of how little I was wearing. "I'll get more."

When Rico went inside, I turned to Satch, who had crushed all the beer cans while I was kissing Rico.

He stared at me, but he wasn't smiling. "I don't know what you're playing at," he said angrily.

"You're the one who wanted us to stop talking about Danny," I shot back.

"So you're in love with Rico now?"

"We're just fooling around." I kicked at his stack of flattened cans, sending them across the yard and startling the moths, which flitted away. "What's so wrong with that?"

"You want to fool around?" Satch stood and grabbed me, his hands clinching my waist. "Okay. Show me what Rico taught you."

"I don't want your kisses." I shoved him hard, but he was huge, his muscled chest like a brick wall, and he didn't budge.

"I thought you needed practice," he joked meanly.

"I'm not going to practice with you." I tried to pull away from him, but he only held me tighter.

"Then consider this the real event," he whispered.

I stared up at him, my eyes widening, as he leaned down. His lips touched mine, hesitating in anticipation of my response. A pleasant ache flowed through me, flooding me with an unbearable yearning. Breathing faster, I wrapped my arms around him and parted my lips, the taste of him overwhelming my senses.

My grandmother had told me that boys were dangerous, but I hadn't understood her warning until Satch kissed me. A hunger awakened within me, causing my heart to race.

When the back door started to open, Satch pushed me away and sat back on the steps.

Dizzy and flushed, I stared at him, wanting another kiss, barely aware of Rico, who stepped outside carrying two new six-packs, which he set on the porch.

He must have felt the tension, because he looked at Satch and then at me. "Did you two have a fight or something?"

Standing, Satch said, "It's been a long day. I'm going to bed."

A sense of hopelessness washed over me as I watched him go inside. Quietly, he closed the door without once glancing back at me. The deadbolt slid into place and then I felt Rico turning me toward him.

"Hey," he whispered, tracing a finger down the front of my blouse before his hands settled on my hips, his smile telling me that he had believed my kiss had been more than it was.

"I'm not ready, Rico," I said softly.

"I'll go slow. Don't worry. I know it's your first time." He leaned closer, his lips tickling my neck as he spoke. "Do you want to go to your house or mine?"

"You don't understand," I said as he started to kiss me. "I don't want to do anything."

He broke away from me, his strained smile not masking his confusion. "But that kiss. What did it mean?"

"I thought you were sad and needed someone to hold you," I confessed, looking down.

"You kissed me because you felt sorry for me?" He swung away from me and slammed his fist into the side of the garage. "I don't want your sympathy."

When he turned back, his expression had hardened.

Instinctively, I backed away.

He grabbed me before I could run. "Just pretend you're luring me for Trek and we'll get along fine." He crushed me against him, his kiss hard.

"Don't!" I cried. When he didn't stop, I bit his lip.

His breathing savage, he pulled back and wiped the blood from his chin.

For a long moment, I just stared at him.

When my breath came in even draws, he offered me his hand. "I'm sorry, Blaise," he said. "Satch is right. It's been a long day. I'll walk you home."

Exhausted, letting my tears flow, I fell against him and felt his arm slip around my waist, his sadness and mine weighing on me as he guided me up the walk to my house.

When I stepped onto my porch, Rico said quietly, "Your kiss made me believe you wanted me." He tapped his chest. "I felt it here. I thought you'd finally fallen in love with me."

I started to tell him that I loved him as a friend, though at the moment, I wasn't even sure about that. He held up his hand to keep me from speaking.

"Don't say anything, Blaise. Just let me talk. I know I was wrong, ugly wrong, in what I tried to do, but I get all this frustration inside me when I'm around you."

After a moment, he spoke without looking at me. "I don't care if I'm only second best. After tonight maybe I'm not even in the running, but the kind of love I'm offering you, most guys aren't willing to give. I'd make you happy. I know I would, and I'd get you out of this neighborhood. We'd live a good life. Just think about what I'm saying."

He finally glanced at me. "Don't be afraid of me. It won't happen again."

He walked away, leaving me alone with a terrible ache in my heart.

I unlocked the door and stepped into the living room.

Ariel sat on the stairs, waiting for me. She stood unsteadily and collapsed against me.

"Danny's in the hospital," she sobbed. "He was almost beaten to death."

22

In disbelief, I stood in the alley where Danny had been beaten, my temples throbbing, the beer sour in my stomach. How could Danny be in intensive care? I had been hit harder and more often during my jump-in. From the length of police tape that cordoned off the lower half of the alley, I reasoned that Danny had almost made his way to Tulley's, but something had happened to him near the sunflowers that lay broken and crushed in the dirt.

Determined to get a closer look, I started forward when I became aware of footsteps crunching the gravel near the street. I ducked behind a rusted-out station wagon as Lobos marched down the alley, beams from their flashlights grazing over the weeds, searching for clues.

When I eased back into the pitch dark near the garages, a familiar hand clasped my elbow, the long fingers warm and squeezing tight. Satch guided me backward.

"Ariel was worried about you," he whispered. "She said you ran off the moment she told you about Danny."

"I should have stayed with her," I said. "But I had to see. I couldn't believe . . . I didn't want to . . . Where is she now?"

"Rico took her home," Satch muttered before rubbing his hands over his face, his anguish rousing my guilt. He hadn't wanted to go after Danny this afternoon; neither had Rico. I had forced them. What would have happened if I hadn't let Trek intimidate me with his pantomime of shooting them? The answer chilled me. I would have found myself standing over a memorial tonight, either Rico's or Satch's.

"Why's Ariel so upset?" Satch asked, pulling me from my thoughts.

"I don't know." I could never tell anyone that she had been seeing Danny.

"She couldn't have known Danny that well," Satch said, prodding for an answer.

"Maybe she just couldn't handle any more violence," I said. "We all knew Danny in elementary school."

"Ariel thinks a doper beat him and stole his drugs," Satch said, holding a side door open. "But that's not possible. Danny was still strong enough to beat off dopers when we left him. Something else happened."

I stepped into the narrow yard that ran between the houses, my bare feet squishing into cold mud. I stopped abruptly on the front lawn near a rusted tricycle.

Across the street, beneath the wispy shadows of an elm tree, Trek waited for us, leaning against his car. Wind ruffled his black sweats and tangled his wet hair, which he had tied loosely at the nape of his neck, giving the impression that he had showered and dressed quickly in a rush to find us.

"Don't say anything," Satch warned, easing beside me.

"Why?" I asked, but Trek had already noticed us, and Satch didn't answer.

"I told you to break Danny's nose, not beat him until he was half-dead," Trek said harshly as we stopped in front of him.

"Danny was sitting up and cursing us," I argued, ignoring Satch, who pressed his hand against my back. "He was strong enough to throw a rock at me before we left him."

Trek glanced at me, his eyes glowing with satisfaction. "Then why is he in intensive care?"

"Something else happened," I said, annoyed with Satch. Why wasn't he defending himself?

Trek grinned. "You might as well take credit for it. No one could have caught Danny without you. You did a good job. Leave it at that."

"We didn't beat him unconscious, so why should I leave it at that?"

"It's up to you." Trek opened the car door. A gun lay on the passenger seat next to three unopened cans of beer. "Right now Lobos are sending a posse into the Borderlands to get the doper they think beat Danny. If they ever learn that he was lured into a beating, they'll come after you."

"How would they find out?" I challenged, every nerve in my body screaming.

"Things like that have a way of getting around," Trek said,

his voice low and ominous. "There are four of us, and you know the old saying 'Four can keep a secret if three are dead.'"

"Then I guess I better practice smiling for my mug shot," I countered as Satch dug his fingers into my back. Too late, I understood his warning not to speak. Trek couldn't have known that we'd actually beaten Danny, but in my haste to defend us, I had confessed.

Trek grinned. "No one's going to call the cops, Blaise. We're going to handle this our own way."

I stared at the taillights as he drove away. The one I had smashed was still not repaired, reminding me of Trek's promise that our game didn't end until I was in love with him.

"Danny's almost dead and Trek's happy about it," I whispered.

"That's because he owns us now," Satch said.

23

Later that night, with insects chirping around me and gunshots echoing from the Borderlands, I sat across the street from Trek's house, deep in the shadows, not wanting Satch to wander by and discover that I had lied to him. I had told him that I was going home to bed when really I planned to talk to Trek and convince him that our beating could not have sent Danny to intensive care.

My plan had seemed reasonable when I'd started out, but the closer I'd gotten to Trek's house, the more my fear had grown. Though I tried to convince myself that my sense of danger was no more than my own imagination, I could not overcome the feeling that if I knocked on his door this late at night, alone, without anyone knowing where I had gone, I would become one of those girls who just disappeared.

From my hiding place, I watched Dante peer out the front window. A moment later, he stepped onto the porch with a cocky stride and looked up and down the street.

I nestled deeper into the weeds, the feathery blades skimming over my face as three more shots fired in the Borderlands. Grisly pictures churned through my mind of what the Lobos would do to me if they ever found out that I had set Danny up.

The murmur of voices drew my attention back across the street. Trek and Omar stepped outside, Melissa with them, dressed in a short black skirt and a sequined top. Her shrieky laughter sent a shock through me. She was high or drunk, and staggered slightly in her platform heels as she danced against Trek, her hands wrapping around his neck. He disentangled himself from her and handed her to Omar.

I felt sickened. I had to decide what to do. I couldn't just let them take her. At the same time, I wondered about my need to rescue her. What exactly was I saving her from? I had no idea where they were going, but it felt wrong.

When I started to stand, a hand clapped over my mouth, startling me. "Don't make a sound. It's me, Kaylee."

I turned so rapidly that for a second her fingers caught in my mouth. "Kaylee? What are you doing here?"

"I told you to be quiet," she whispered. "What do you think I'm doing? I came here hoping to figure out a way to get even with Trek. I know where he hides his extra key and I keep hoping he'll leave the house unguarded so I can go inside and trash it."

A bolt of excitement rushed through me. "Where's the key?" I asked.

Her eyes widened and she pointed across the street. "Will you shut up?" she asked in a barely audible voice as she crouched lower.

Omar was staring at the weed-infested shadows where we sat, his hand at his waistband ready to draw his Beretta. I froze. He'd fire first and investigate later, but Trek said something and Omar's hand fell to his side. He opened the front car door and waited for Melissa to sit on the passenger's seat.

Kaylee pinched my arm. "You won't be able to talk Melissa into leaving Trek, anyway. I've tried."

"You have?" I glanced back at Kaylee, stunned.

"I told her that I'd been with Trek, but she called me a liar," Kaylee explained. "So I talked to Ariel. I thought maybe she could convince Melissa that I was telling the truth."

"Why didn't you ask me? Maybe I could have—"

"Melissa would never listen to you," Kaylee interrupted.

"Why not?"

"She's too jealous of you since Trek asked you to be the lure."

I wanted to feel surprised about this, but I wasn't. I glanced back across the street as Trek slid behind the steering wheel. Melissa sat in the front, laughing loudly and dancing with her hands, while Omar climbed into the rear. Dante gave one more look around, then went back inside.

"This isn't like Melissa," I whispered.

"You can't blame her," Kaylee said. "Trek has a way of filling your head until you don't have room for your own thoughts. When I was seeing him, he told me that I couldn't let anyone find out that we were a couple because if his enemies knew, they'd try to kill me. He even convinced me the bullets that took out Gabriella were meant for me."

"And you believed him?"

"Sure. He has this power, Blaise. He can make you believe anything, and now he's got Melissa under that spell."

I thought of the conversation I had overheard between Trek and Melissa when they'd been sitting on her stoop. He had said that she was the one who had wanted to do the rollins. Had he been planting the thought in her mind to make her believe that the rollins had been her choice, when really it had been his way of breaking her, so he could put her back together into a completely different person?

"How did you escape him?" I asked as the car engine started and the headlights came on.

"He got me pregnant."

I clutched her hand. I hadn't known. "Oh, Kaylee, you should have told me."

"I thought Trek would be happy," Kaylee said, her eyes glinting with tears. "He wasn't. He told me I had to fix the problem, but I'd already named the baby Isabella. No way was I going to harm her. I lost her, anyway," she said bitterly. "After I'd miscarried, Trek started telling me how much he'd wanted the baby. He blamed me for losing her and kept asking me what I'd done wrong. But I'd loved Isabella too much for him to be able to convince me that it was my fault. That's when I started realizing what he was doing to me."

The car sped away, music blaring, the thudding beat setting off the alarms in the cars parked along the street.

"Do you know where they're going?" I asked.

"To a party," Kaylee said, her gaze far away, as if memories were coming back to her.

"This late?"

"They wait until the other girls have gone home," Kaylee said. "He's been passing Melissa around to his friends."

"How do you know?" I asked, feeling more queasy than angry.

"Because he did it to me."

2A

The expectation that Trek was going to use Danny's beating to blackmail me was taking its toll. I couldn't sleep and, when I did, the dreams tormented me. I spent my nights with Satch and Rico, watching scary movies and drinking beer until I drifted off, Rico always soothing me when I jolted awake.

On this night, almost two weeks after the beating, I broke out of a nightmare, my fingers outstretched, grasping for the boy. The arms enfolding me tightened around me, the tenderness in the touch reassuring me that I was safe. Even so, a curious tension kept me bound to the dream. I scanned Satch's bedroom, expecting to see blood splattered across the walls, which fluttered with light from the muted TV.

In the dream, the boy had come back to life, his pallid skin shimmering. He'd looked surprised to find himself alive and had walked toward me, through the pools of blood, his steps making wet, sopping sounds.

The killer's coming, he'd warned me. *The killer's coming after you.*

"The dream felt so real," I whispered.

"I tried to wake you." The drowsy voice at my ear made me flinch. Satch had his arms around me, not Rico. "When I couldn't get you to wake up, I just held you the way Rico does."

I nodded, trying to understand the sensations rippling through me. The closeness of Satch's body stole my ability to breathe. Something slipped across my abdomen. I glanced down. Satch's hand rested on my stomach. Was he even aware of how tightly he had pressed himself against me?

"Where's Rico?" I asked, sounding frantic and startling Satch, who had fallen half-asleep.

"Bombing the Lobos' neighborhood with paint," Satch said.

I nodded, feeling responsible. Defacing their *placas*, getting the adrenaline rush when they came after him, was his way to get rid of his frustration over me.

"Get some sleep," Satch murmured.

I twisted in his arms until I could see his eyes. "Why don't you and Rico have bad dreams?"

"Who says we don't?" His gaze held mine, the streetlight soft on his face. "Do you think I don't relive breaking Danny's nose? No one escapes the memories. You just learn to endure them." His eyes closed. "Go back to sleep."

I buried my head against his chest.

"Relax, Blaise," Satch whispered. "Nothing is going to happen while I've got you."

As his hands stroked me, warmth flooded through me. My muscles loosened and I snuggled against him, enjoying the feel of his body so close to mine.

I hadn't been aware of drifting off until gray light awakened me. Satch was still sleeping, his arms encircling me. Gently, I lifted myself on top of him and placed my lips on his. His eyes opened.

"Good morning," I whispered.

"What are you doing?" he asked, instantly pushing away from me and looking around the room as if searching for Rico.

"Sorry. I thought . . . you know, after last night . . ." I crawled off him, embarrassment raging inside me. I was furious with myself for showing him how I felt.

I jumped off the bed, knocking over a stack of library books, aware that Satch was still watching me with an apologetic expression in his eyes. Struggling to conceal my hurt, I slipped into my shoes and dodged from his room, tears making a prism of my vision.

"I'll catch you at school," I yelled too cheerily.

Satch called after me, but I refused to turn back and let him see me cry. When I heard his steps slapping the floorboards behind me, I rushed down the stairs and out into the cool morning.

At home, I showered, scrubbing my skin, trying to wash away my humiliation. How was I ever going to face Satch again? I dressed, my hair still wet, and took a roundabout way to school, only to pause a few blocks later.

Someone had cut through the coils of razor wire at the top of the fence that enclosed an abandoned building. A long loop dangled free, the blades scratching across the sidewalk, the glittering metal teeth tempting children to investigate.

The graffiti on the building told me who had done this. *Lobos* was sprayed above *Que hora es, Rico?* The question asked the time, but to any gangster the meaning was clear: *You're going to die, Rico.* His time was up. To emphasize this, a target sight encircled his name.

At the moment, the carelessness angered me more than the threat. Didn't anyone care about the little kids who played around here? I picked up the razor wire and threw it back into the rolls overhead. Then, taking deep breaths, I pulled myself together and walked away, my expression hardening as I neared school.

In the hallway, while I was searching for Rico, I felt someone coming up behind me fast. I turned as Twyla and Tanya shoved me into the bathroom that Core 9 claimed. Tara sauntered in after them, lighting a new cigarette off the ember in her old one, which she tossed into the sink.

"You've got a problem," Tara said, smoke leaking from her mouth. "And it's only going to get worse unless you take my advice."

My heart slammed against my ribs, certain she had learned about Danny. Or maybe the boy.

"You can't be with two guys at the same time," she said.

"Two?" I countered, my mind so focused on murder and bloodshed that it took me a moment to understand she was talking about Satch and Rico. "I'm not even with one."

"I told you she'd deny it," Twyla said.

"You've been spending the night with Satch and Rico," Tara said, matter-of-factly.

"We just hang out. We don't do anything," I said emphatically, certain I knew where this was going.

"Core 9 girls do not give it up to boys that way." Tara drew on the cigarette until the ember glowed red. "We're tough. We fight. We use guys. They don't use us."

I stammered, not sure if I could explain, not sure if I even wanted to try, when Melissa, who rarely came to school anymore, burst into the restroom. A new tattoo started in a curlicue leaf on her ankle and looped sinuously around and up her leg in a vine of flowers. She hesitated when she saw the 3Ts glaring at her.

"This is a private bathroom," Twyla said, sauntering toward the door. "You're not allowed in here anymore."

"That's the only warning you're going to get." Tanya bumped against Melissa in a show of disrespect.

Indifferent to the despair on Melissa's face, Tara flicked her cigarette at her. "You made yourself a trash can for guys, so what do you expect?"

After the 3Ts left, Melissa kept her eyes downcast.

"Hey," I said softly. "Are you okay?"

"Something bad's going on with Trek," Melissa whispered without taking her gaze off the cigarette burning on the floor. "It's not the usual crazy stuff. This is different."

"I believe you," I said, slipping my arm around her.

Though Melissa didn't know the cause of Trek's mood, I did. The reward for information leading to the arrest of the person responsible for killing the eleven-year-old boy had skyrocketed to $100,000. Civilians hadn't cared that Nando had died, but the kid's death had outraged them. The story still made the news, the reward growing as people held rallies.

"Melissa?" I asked when her silence had gone on for too long.

"I want out," she whispered.

"You want out of Core 9?" I didn't understand the problem. No one was going to stop her. I doubted that anyone would even care.

"The things I'm doing scare me."

I froze. "Like what?"

She was silent, fidgeting, as if trying to decide how much she should tell me. "Trek and I have this game. At first, it was just to help me get over my shyness."

"You've never been shy," I started, then stopped. "Tell me about the game."

"He picks a guy at random and tells me to flirt with him."

I felt a shiver of apprehension. "Why does he do that?"

She smiled slightly. "I think he likes to see the way guys are attracted to me."

"And that scares you?"

"That doesn't, but Trek keeps changing the game. Now he wants to see how many guys I have to ask on a date before I can get one to say yes."

"Are the guys his friends?"

She shook her head. "Strangers. Business types, like, at the convention center."

A sick, oily feeling slipped into my stomach as I imagined the old men in suits waiting in a taxi line. How many did Melissa have to ask before one said yes? Not many, I guessed. "And?"

"When I get a yes," Melissa continued, "then I run back to Trek and we laugh about it. But the last couple of times, Trek's disappeared and left me stranded."

"Then what?"

"I go on the date." She chewed on the end of her nail until a thin line of blood appeared.

I stared at the greenish-blue mark encircling her wrist.

"Did Trek do that to you?" I took her hand, the skin greasy with lotions that smelled of lavender and mint, and gently pushed up her sleeve. Fingerprint bruises dotted her arm.

"I told you something really bad has put him in a foul mood. Nothing I do makes him happy anymore. Not even the games."

"Let's ditch school and go someplace where we can talk," I said.

"I can't." She pulled her hand away, leaving a residue of lotion on my palm. "Trek's waiting for me outside. I just didn't want the 3Ts to hear what he asked me to tell you."

Panic shot through me.

"He wants you to go over to his house after school today, dressed up." She leaned against the exit door. "And bring Satch and Rico with you."

"Melissa," I pleaded, "don't go back to Trek."

"I'm okay. Really. I shouldn't have told you about the games. I knew you'd make too much out of them. Trek just wants me to come out of my shell and be a party girl. What's wrong with that?"

"It doesn't sound like you."

"What's me anymore?" The emptiness behind her smile broke my heart. She pushed against the door and left me alone in the bathroom.

After composing myself, I headed down the empty hall, then went outside and started toward the dead-end street near the Borderlands in search of Rico and Satch. I was so lost in my own thoughts that it took me a moment to register the chaos at the side of the school. Students who should have been crowding the hallways stood in tight clusters, smiling and nodding and laughing at the graffiti that covered the wall. Even a *clica* of Lobos girls gaped at the artwork, hiding their smiles from Gatita, who looked furious.

Painted across the bricks was a caricature of Danny, *el rompe-corazones*, cowering in front of a pudgy little cupid, who was shooting arrows at him. Red hearts bubbled around vivid yellow zigzagged letters that spelled out *El Cobarde*, the coward. Below that were the words *Temerozo de amor*, fearful of love, and the last line read *Que miedoso es*, how scared he is. I recognized Ariel's style and glanced around.

She was leaning against the wire mesh fence near the parking lot, admiring the graffiti, apparently not concerned about the cops, security guards, and teachers who were threading their way around the students, checking hands for paint stains, as they hunted for the tagger who had defaced school property.

"Nice work." I said, joining her.

"Kaylee helped me," Ariel said. She guided her fingernails under her eyes to catch her mascara-stained tears. "We had to throw it up fast before the security guards made their rounds. She's pretty good."

"Yeah," I agreed. "It looks great."

"I wish she'd told me all that bit about Trek when it was going on," Ariel said. "It makes me sick the way I treated her right when she needed me most."

"None of us were there for her because we were so worried about our own reputations," I said, but I didn't think that was the reason Ariel was crying. "What did Danny do to deserve all the paint?"

"He broke up with me," Ariel explained, her tears spilling faster than she could wipe them away.

My heart seized. "He's conscious?"

She nodded. "They moved him out of intensive care, and when I snuck into the hospital to see him—"

"Did he tell you what had happened?" I broke in anxiously.

"He's too scared," Ariel said. "He won't talk to the cops or his homies. And he told me it's too dangerous for us to continue seeing each other. He was actually shaking, like he was afraid someone was going to walk into the room and catch us together. He asked me to leave."

That didn't sound like Danny, who was normally fearless. He had even threatened me. Something had happened after we left him that had terrified him into silence. He wasn't the kind of guy who would back down to protect himself. He was doing this for Ariel.

"It was risky, Ariel," I said finally. "The two of you could have been shot for seeing each other."

"But I want a guy who's willing to risk bullets to be with me." She let out a long sigh as I held her against me.

"What's one more heartbreak?" she said. "I've had so many. It's just that this time it feels like I won't survive it."

"You will," I said, rubbing her back.

Though I felt responsible for her tears, I also felt relief. I was safe from Danny. Now, my only threat came from Trek, which was bad enough. I had to find a way to free us all from him.

25

That afternoon I sat on the floor in Trek's living room, wearing thigh-pinching jeans and a zippered jacket that covered the lacy bra I intended to expose when I lured Trek's target. Resting against my legs, Pixie and Bonnie whimpered and licked my fingers, seeming aware of the apprehension and anger brewing inside me. I scratched behind their ears, keeping my hands busy so no one could see the tremor in my fingers.

Barely breathing, his face blank, Rico leaned against the wall while Satch sat in a straight-backed chair, fingers tight on his knees, ready to catapult himself into an attack, his eyes locked on Trek. Dante stood sentinel at the window, his focus beyond the glass on the street.

Trek sat in the chair closest to me, his excitement palpable, which troubled me more than if I had sensed the dark mood that Melissa had described. His bare feet, scrupulously clean, rested on the coffee table next to a handgun. The stainless steel barrel caught the overhead light, the reflection stabbing my eyes every time I glanced up at Satch, who avoided my gaze.

Finally, Trek spoke. "I want you to go over to the Pentagon Mall. Tony works there after school, on the third floor, store three twenty-three. Don't kill, just wound. Don't try for the arm. It's too close to the head. Shoot low, the knee, the leg. Can you manage that?"

"Who couldn't?" Rico said, deflecting the insult.

I tried to picture a drug dealer working out of a store in the shopping center. Maybe a teen who lived a double life, addicted to the thrill of selling illegal drugs while maintaining an honor student image. Such a guy would be easy to lure.

Trek picked up the handgun and offered it to Rico, who took it and checked the sights, the bore, the barrel, before rotating the cylinder. "There's only one bullet in the chamber," Rico said.

"After the way you exploded on Danny, I can't trust you with a fully loaded weapon," Trek replied.

Rico remained silent, his face stone, but even so his anger bristled into the room. For a moment, I thought he was going to use the bullet on Trek.

Dante pulled away from the window and stepped into the line of fire, easing the tension. "I got something for you." From his back pocket, he pulled out an object that looked like a short pipe. I recognized it immediately as a homemade silencer. He took the gun from Rico and, after clicking on the safety, twisted the silencer onto the barrel.

"And to show you that we're cool," Trek said, "I'm going to give you each a hundred dollars for the job." The amount, so small, was an insult, another way to say he owned us. He nodded toward Dante. "Pay them."

Grinning, Dante pulled a roll of twenties from his side pocket and, counting out five bills, walked over to Satch, who held up his hand, refusing payment. Rico stared at Trek, not even acknowledging Dante, who then stepped past him to me. Though I desperately needed the money, I ignored Dante, too. He left the twenties on the coffee table and returned to his post at the window.

"It's all on the three of you, now," Trek said, releasing us.

I didn't feel good about this. The bullet was going to cripple Tony, but I didn't see a way around it, either. I kissed the puppies good-bye, letting them nuzzle my face, then got up and followed Satch and Rico to the door.

Halfway there, Dante stepped in front of me, blocking my way, as Trek stood, scooped the money off the coffee table, and stuffed it into my purse.

"I owe you for taking care of my dogs." He closed my purse before I could object, and then his hands strayed to my waist. In a voice too quiet for anyone but me to hear, he added, "Are you still playing hard to get?"

"I hate what you're doing to Melissa," I countered.

"She likes what she does," he said.

"Have you convinced her that it's fun?" I tried to get away from him, but his fingers hooked onto the waistband of my low-cut jeans and pulled me off balance. I fell against him.

"You sound like you're jealous of all the attention I've been giving her." The seriousness in his eyes sent a shock through me. "You are, aren't you?"

"You wish," I sneered.

"You should give me a try," he said, releasing me. "I could be good for you."

I said nothing, my heart thudding, and started around him.

"Does your silence mean you want me, or are you trying to tell me that you're done with me?" He laughed.

I shoved past him, ignoring his laughter and the warning in the back of my mind that I would never be done with Trek. This was only the beginning.

26

The greasy smoke from the hamburger grill swept over us the moment Satch, Rico, and I stepped from the Metro station into the food court at the bottom of the mall. Shoppers mobbed the eating area, utensils and trays clattering, as they jammed in line at the fast food counters and ate packed together at the long tables. Their voices echoed into the atrium and filled the shopping center with a frantic hum that set my nerves on edge.

I followed Satch onto the escalator, Rico behind me. The tread boards hitched and jerked, straining under the weight of so many passengers. I hadn't expected the mall to be this crowded.

On the third floor, we stopped near the entrance to store 323. I stared at the cashmere sweaters in the window display. "No druggie is going to wear those clothes."

"That doesn't mean the guy working inside isn't selling," Satch said.

Rico peered through the glass, oblivious to the shoppers jostling around him, his hand under his shirt on the gun. "I don't see Tony. Maybe he's in the back."

"I'll go in." I unzipped my jacket, exposing my bra and flat stomach, the top of my jeans two inches below my hipbones. I strolled inside, swinging my purse and smiling, though I could barely breathe.

A girl with long blonde extensions stood behind a counter, folding purple sweaters. She looked delicate and vulnerable, almost prim, in a long-sleeved blouse and pink skirt that she'd obviously purchased in this store.

"Hi!" The eagerness in her greeting suggested that she had been waiting all afternoon for a customer. "Can I help you?"

I ignored her and scanned the rows of dresses, expecting to see furtive movement in the pastel colors. Where the hell was Tony?

"Are you alone?" I stepped over to the girl, surprised to see piercings in her brow, nose, and lips that she had tried to conceal under foundation. Maybe the store owner didn't allow her to wear hardware to work.

"We're meeting our friend here." Rico's voice came from behind me.

"He's supposed to be working the afternoon shift," Satch added.

"I'm the only one clocked in." The girl folded the sweater against her chest, her gaze locked on Satch, who took her stare as an invitation. He eased around the counter.

"Maybe you know where we can find him," Satch said, his smile irresistible.

She shrugged. "I'm new here, so I don't know all the employees."

Leaning down, Satch read her nametag and then glanced up at me. His somber expression told me something was wrong.

"Hey, Tony," he murmured, focusing in on the girl again. "I like your name."

Cursing, Rico grabbed my hand and pulled me through the racks of new-smelling clothes to the men's section.

"Tony?" I whispered in shock, staring at Rico. "She's Tony?"

"We were gunning for a drug dealer," Rico said. "You don't build a reputation shooting schoolgirls." He snatched a fedora off a male mannequin.

I caught the plastic body before it toppled and set it upright while Rico tore the price tag off the brim.

"Trek must be tripping." Rico set the hat on his head. "I'm not going to shoot her. What could she have done, anyway, blown him off at some party?"

"Someone gave him the wrong information," I said. "He wouldn't have sent me along if he'd known Tony was a girl."

"He knew," Rico contended. "No way Trek didn't know."

"But why would he let us believe she was a guy?" I asked.

"He was having fun, gaming us." Rico ripped a tweed jacket off its hanger and pulled out his pocketknife. "I'm not taking care of his sorry love life. Does he think I'm an errand boy like Dante?"

Tony looked up, her gaze shifting to Rico, who was cutting the security sensor from the jacket seam. "Are you going to buy that?" she asked.

The authority that she had mustered into her voice renewed my interest in her. Who was she? She looked familiar, but I still couldn't place her.

"Why else would I take off the theft detector?" Rico replied, tossing the gray plastic tab onto the floor before sliding his arms into the sleeves.

Convinced that Rico was going to pay, Tony turned back to Satch, her eyes glimmering with fascination.

I wondered if I'd seen her at a club. Some high school girls liked to pick up on gangsters for a night of danger before they returned to their safe homes. More likely, Tony only resembled the ones that I'd watched flirt with Rico and Satch. All good girls looked alike to me with their bright smiles and bouncy hair.

I trudged over to Rico. "Don't steal anything," I said in a harsh whisper. "If the security guards catch you, they'll find the gun."

"I'm going to end up in jail if I don't get killed first, so what does it matter?"

"It matters to me," I argued before Satch's voice pulled me back to what he was saying to Tony.

"Jump out of here with me," Satch murmured to Tony, his thigh pressed against the counter. "I'll buy you a coffee, one of those sweet mocha things."

Tony giggled, trapped between desire and fear.

"You drink coffee, don't you?" Satch bent closer, blocking her view of the exit.

"I love coffee," she admitted, her blush deepening, as Rico strutted out of the store, wearing the tweed jacket and fedora while waving to the surveillance camera.

I plucked the price tags off the floor and, fanning them for the same camera, carried them up to the checkout counter. I wasn't going to let Rico get arrested. "I need to check out!"

Tony blinked, seeming surprised to find herself at work.

"Go ahead and take care of business," Satch said smoothly. "I'll catch you later."

"Promise?" she asked shyly.

"Promise," he said before he left to join Rico.

Tony stepped over to the cash register, the red fading from her cheeks. "I like your friend," she confided as she took the tags. "He seems really sweet."

The happiness radiating from her smile annoyed me. "Can you just hurry?" I said, more harshly than I had intended.

"Sorry," she whispered.

After she scanned the tags, I paid with the money that Trek had stashed in my purse, then took my receipt and change and left.

Rico and Satch were waiting near the entrance. Their conversation stopped when I joined them, but the remnants of their anger hung in the air, and I knew they had been discussing Trek.

"What did you do with the clothes?" I asked Rico, who was no longer wearing the jacket or the hat.

"Do you think I want to get arrested?" He teased and pointed inside. "I took them back."

The clothes lay under the counter where Tony had been folding sweaters. His theft had been a ruse so he and Satch could talk without me, which made me fume.

"That is so not funny," I said, trying to swallow the anger that tightened my throat. "I'm not laughing, Rico."

"Go get your refund," Satch said, nudging me back to the store.

I stepped inside and, as I started to pick up the clothes,

I glanced at Tony, who was leaning against the cash register, reading a store flyer. Her hair extensions fell into her face and, when she lifted her hand to brush them back, the stars tattooed around her wrist peeked out from her cuff.

Cold panic settled into my stomach as my eyes darted to her brow, nose, and lips, and I imagined silver hoops in her piercings, her hair cut short and colored black.

Before she saw me, I dodged back to Satch and Rico.

"Tony was the cashier the night Trek killed Nando and the boy."

Their eyes shot back to Tony, who looked up and waved, unaware of how close she had come to spending the night in a hospital emergency room.

"You never saw the cashier's face," Satch said to me. "So how can you be sure?"

"That night, I saw the stars tattooed around her wrist. The same design is inked into Tony's skin."

"Lots of girls probably have that tattoo," Rico said, studying her with renewed interest.

"I know she was the cashier. She's trying to change her appearance. She might not have seen the killer, but she knows the killer saw her, and she's terrified. How did Trek find her? The news never mentioned her name or anything that could have identified her."

"It would have been easy for Trek to find out who was working the late shift that night," Satch said. "But after all this time, why'd he even bother?"

"The reward money has him worried," I said. "He sent us on

this mission so we could prove our commitment to him by shoot-ing Tony."

"Is Trek totally insane?" Rico asked angrily. "If we shot Tony, cops would never stop looking for us."

"Our word should have been enough," Satch said. "We left our fingerprints all over that rifle."

We stared at each other, a thousand questions unspoken.

Satch and Rico had been dressed like church boys that night, and I'd worn a mix of sexy clothes and my school uniform. We'd been wet, our hair plastered to our scalps. But maybe Tony had got-ten a good look at one of us even though we hadn't seen her face.

I flinched. "We have to get out of here before Tony figures out who we are. She's probably got a detective on speed dial."

27

The gloom inside the Metro station reinforced my bleak mood. Even Satch looked subdued, his face bloodless and drawn in the gray light. Only Rico, who walked ahead of us, seemed unaffected by the murkiness. We rode the escalator down to the platform and, there, in the stuttering light from the windows of a passing train, stood Babo, a hard-core Lobo, part of the *locos* crew.

He smiled up at us, his black trench coat billowing in the slipstream. The *vato* with him was a stranger to me, but the prison tattoos on his neck and shaved head read like a biography that told me he had killed once, served time for robbery but not the murder, and his gang name was Joker. His wide grin let me know he had the *locura*.

"They're fools to challenge us here," I said, though my real warning was for Rico. Toughness was a virtue, but you didn't act like a killer inside the Metro, where transit police loomed in the tunnels, ready for a throwdown. Moreover, you didn't do it with only one bullet in your gun.

Rico ignored me and strode over to Babo, the slowness in his stride showing he wasn't afraid.

"Hey, *ese*," Rico said, mocking Babo's accent. "What are you doing so far from your *barrio*?"

"Looking for a *baile*," Babo said, his smile fierce. He didn't mean a dance. He was looking for a fight.

The whir of brakes filled the tunnel and the floor lights flashed red as another train arrived. The color pulsed over Babo, who lifted his coat to flaunt the automatic weapon hidden at his side. Though powerful, the gun was a distraction. The real threat came from Joker, who was pulling a pistol from his coat.

Undaunted, Rico lifted his shirt and gripped the gun handle while Satch slipped his hand into his jacket, pretending to reach for a gun.

The train stopped, its doors opened, and passengers swarmed in and out, skimming past each other and clogging the firing field. The Lobos let their coats close, concealing their weapons as they watched Rico and Satch, who dropped their hands to their sides in a momentary truce.

With the crowd still passing in front of them, Satch said something to Rico and, though I couldn't hear the exchange, I knew what they were planning and braced myself.

The moment the computer voice announced that the train doors were closing, Satch and Rico spun around, grabbed my arms, lifting me between them, and carried me on board. The doors swished together, the rubber edges brushing over my shoes before Babo and Joker could react.

I leaned against Satch, my heart thundering. "I hate it when you guys do that. Can't you just yell, 'Run!'?"

"Not as much fun," he teased, his attention turning to Babo, who raced alongside our window.

Babo flashed our gang sign, adding a vulgar gesture and, before Rico could send a message back, the train sped into the tunnel.

Passengers, believing the exchange had been nothing serious, settled into the train's motion, opening books and newspapers and scrolling through messages on their cell phones.

I took a seat and slid over to make room for Satch, who walked past me and leaned against a pole. Rico sat next to me, took my purse, opened it, and dropped his hand inside.

"You've got to be more careful with the hammer," he said, rearranging it. "You don't want the claw to snag on something when you pull it out in a fight."

"You're expecting more trouble?" I asked.

"Do you think Babo was at the station because he wanted to go shopping?"

I shook my head. "He wasn't surprised to see us so far from our neighborhood, and he should have been. Someone told him we'd be there."

"Trek did."

"Why?"

Without answering my question, Rico zipped my purse, set it on the floor in front of me, and eased his arm around me, his face against mine, not kissing me, but seeming to breathe in my essence.

"I'm not afraid of dying, Blaise," he whispered, "but I don't want to leave you. I'm going to miss you so damn much."

I pulled back so I could look at him. "You're worrying me. Please don't do something stupid, like another suicide raid into Lobos territory, just because Babo—"

"Promise me you won't hate me after you find out how selfish I've been."

"What are you talking about?"

"Give me that, at least."

"I could never hate you."

"Promise?"

"I promise, but tell me what you're planning."

"Don't forget this," he said, leaning back and closing his eyes.

The train swerved and started its descent under the Potomac River. The friction between the rails and wheels created a shrill screech that stopped all conversation. I wanted to shake the smile off Rico's face and nag him until he told me his plan, but I couldn't question him more unless I shouted over the train's noise, which would be loud enough for all the passengers to hear.

I stared at our reflection in the window, afraid that Rico was seeing death as his only way out. Some homies got to that crazy, reckless place when they stopped caring if they lived or died. But the death wish was never really about wanting to die. It was about wanting to escape this life and be free from the hate and violence forever.

28

Plastic bags, caught in the fence and battered by the wind, had stretched into long gray streamers that snapped over our heads when Satch, Rico, and I stopped in the darkness near Tulley's. The furtive sound of footsteps rushing through the grass had awakened my gangster sixth sense. I tiptoed through the dead weeds near a fire hydrant and peered back down the street in search of shadows that didn't blend into the night and, though I saw nothing, the impression of danger didn't leave me.

Unexpectedly, Rico raced up the sidewalk ahead of us and jumped on the stoop of a row house. Bluish light from the TV screen flickered in the windows, the glow flashing over him.

"What's he doing?" I asked Satch, who stood beside me. "Doesn't he feel it? You do, don't you?"

Satch nodded. "Someone's been following us since we left the Metro station."

"Why doesn't Rico sense it?"

"He does. That's why he's making himself a target."

Terror shuddered through me. "Rico!"

He was already racing back to us, clinging to the shadows, concealing himself behind low-hanging branches and tall weeds that shimmered in the breeze.

"If they don't want to shoot us, then what do they want?" Rico asked when he joined us again.

"We need to find out who they are before we can figure that out," Satch said.

"Maybe it's a pack of dopers," I whispered.

Satch touched my shoulder, cautioning me to listen.

The three of us waited, becoming still. Minutes passed, and then, a lonesome, high-pitched howl echoed into the night. Other voices joined in, coming from several directions, the desolate songs of wolves that didn't belong in a city. Lobos called their haunting cries *gritando*. They were surrounding us and wanted us to know that we'd soon feel their bullets.

"We didn't escape them," Satch said, a trace of surprise in his voice. "One of their homies must have boarded the train at the mall and called the others when we got off near here."

"This is creepy," I said as the wails continued to pervade the dark.

Rico smiled slyly. "They won't look for us in their own neighborhood. I know a place."

I glanced at Satch, unsure about hiding out in Lobos territory.

"We can't stay here," he said, ducking low and pulling me with him. "They'll close in on us soon."

We slipped into the shadows, letting the night enshroud us,

and stole east toward the Anacostia River. Satch curled his arm around me as we followed Rico through a narrow passageway where homeless men slouched against the walls.

Near a loading dock behind a small grocery store, we entered the Lobos' neighborhood, where rival gang members from Mass 5 had crossed out the Lobos' graffiti and had written their own inscriptions, claiming the alley belonged to them.

"Lobos must have caught Mass 5 before they finished tagging," Satch said, pointing to the bullet holes in the bricks.

"They left their paint when they ran." Rico picked up one of the cans that littered the ground and pressed the nozzle. A spray of gold hissed into the air.

Satch waved the mist away. "Dump the paint."

"I got plans." Rico gathered more cans and, clutching them in his arms, led us into the courtyard of an apartment complex where a mural memorialized the Lobos' homeboys. I read the roll call of the dead. Some I had known, boys my age and younger.

"Hide," Rico whispered.

Though I had heard nothing, I trusted his instincts and eased into a brightly lit alcove, the entrance to someone's home. Moths batted my hand as I gripped the light bulb, the heat searing my fingers, and unscrewed it from its socket.

Moments later, footsteps scuffed down the sidewalk. Three gangbangers strolled past me, dressed alike in bagged-out khaki work pants. They had slit open the long pant legs to free their feet for running, and eight inches of excess material dragged on the concrete behind their shoes. They continued on, unaware that their enemy had ventured so deep into their homeland. The one nearest me had his gun out, held at his side, ready to fire.

I left the light bulb on the doormat, my fingers stinging, and met Satch and Rico in the courtyard. We crept onward, spread far apart this time, three targets instead of one, down yet another alley and onto a vacant lot that was used as an illegal dump site, next to an abandoned factory on the banks of the Anacostia River.

"We'll be safe here," Rico said. "Lobos only patrol this area once a night, usually near dawn."

On the side of the factory, Lobos had painted *Rifamos*, bragging that they were unsurpassed, the fiercest gangsters in Washington, D.C. The closing inscription, *P/V*, was an abbreviation of *por vida*, their promise to rule this part of the District forever.

Paint vapors settled over me, cold in the night air, as Rico began blotting out the Lobos' graffiti with black paint.

"They're already gunning for you, Rico," I said. "Can't you just leave it?"

"Impossible," he explained. "I got to show Babo that he can't hit me up and get away with it."

"It could cost you your life. Is it worth it?"

Grinning, he pulled the neck of his T-shirt up over his nose and began spraying gold paint.

I slogged through the knee-deep trash toward Satch, who sat on the end of a weathered wharf. The smaller rats scuttled away from my footsteps, but the larger ones ignored my intrusion and continued gnawing on chicken bones and apple cores.

Near the river, the smells of tar and mud replaced the sour

garbage odor. When I crossed the wharf, the wood planks rasped and sagged beneath my steps, sounding close to breaking.

"Big day, huh?" I said, sitting beside Satch, careful where I set my purse.

"It doesn't get worse than this," he assured me, sensing the anxiety behind my smile. "This is the bottom."

I nodded, my body starting to relax as I listened to the water lap at the piles. I glanced at Satch and caught him watching me. The way he was looking at me was messing with my head. Was he smiling to encourage me? I touched his arm and let my fingers linger.

Instantaneously, he shifted away, my hand dropping between us as he glanced back at Rico, who was still spraying paint. Satch turned back and stared out at the trash floating downstream.

"You're always running away from me," I whispered, not even sure he could hear me over the water.

"I never mean to hurt you, Blaise. I swear. That's all you need to know."

"No, that's not enough," I said, clenching the edge of the wharf for support. "You and Rico taught me to trust my gut, because that was the only way to survive. Do you know what my instincts are telling me right now?"

"Don't say it, Blaise," he said without looking at me.

"Why?" I demanded.

He turned abruptly, startling me, his eyes fierce when he stared into mine. "It can't be more than friendship. I'm sorry, but it will never be more than that." He glanced back at the warehouse. "Damn."

He jumped up, the wharf swaying precariously, and ran back to Rico. I thought he was deserting me the way he always did, until the hum of a car engine became louder than the sloshing river.

Lobos, I thought, grabbing my purse. I stood, a rush of air escaping my lungs. Rico had painted his name in shimmering gold letters across the factory wall. He was going to take a bullet for what he'd done.

I raced back to the lot in time to see a black Cadillac Escalade turn the corner. My heart slid into my stomach. Rico was running toward the car.

"Get down!" I shouted.

The Cadillac trounced over the curb. An explosion of noise followed, roaring against my ears, as the tires ground through the debris and split open trash bags. Papers spiraled behind the rear bumper, rising into the air.

The headlights burst over Rico, who aimed his one-bullet gun at the car speeding toward him.

29

Abruptly, the car swerved again, swaying from side to side, over metal pipes and broken chunks of concrete. The front bumper hit a rusted shopping cart, catapulting it into a thicket of black trash bags. Satch reached Rico first and stood transfixed beside him as a kaleidoscope of glass from beer and whiskey bottles sprayed from the car's back tires.

I jumped over a discarded washing machine and joined them, my lungs heaving.

"It's Trek and Dante," Rico said, letting the gun fall to his side.

Less than twenty feet away, the car stopped. The driver's side door opened and Dante slid out, a cigarette clenched between his teeth. Smoke swirled from his mouth and nose, clouding his face. He ambled around to the front of the car, his hand smoothing over the hood.

"You like this beauty I jacked?" he asked, oblivious to our tension as he opened the car door for Trek, who turned, his gaze falling on Satch.

"You've disappointed me, Baby Rex," Trek said, his voice menacing. "I thought you would have been smarter than to hole up in enemy territory like your dad. This was the first place I came looking for you."

Satch returned Trek's gaze straight on but said nothing.

Dante finally understood that we were making a stand. He flicked his cigarette into the trash and shrank back to the car bumper, a coward who would be loyal to the winning side.

Trek bailed from the car and strode toward us, his shoes crashing over splintered boards. "I want to know why there was no shooting at the mall. I should have seen pandemonium on TV, a mall evacuated after a gun was fired, but all I saw was the price of gasoline."

His smile told me that one of us was going to die even before I heard the *rack-rack* of a pump-action shotgun. He swung the twenty-gauge, pistol-grip shotgun up and aimed it at us. The barrel had been sawed off and altered, the flash guard removed.

My stomach turned to ice.

"You used to be my favorites," Trek continued, "and now I have to kill one of you, otherwise everyone's going to think it's okay to back out on me."

Rico tensed his grip on the gun.

"You think you can take me?" Trek challenged, excited, easing his shotgun down to his side until he and Rico were faced off, waiting for the other to draw.

Trek had dropped his shotgun too readily. Did Rico's gun even work? "Tony's not a threat to you, Trek." I interrupted their standoff. "Only a fool would want to shoot a schoolgirl who—"

"Are you calling me a fool?" Trek jammed the gun into my chest, knocking me back. The pain stunned me.

"The eleven-year-old boy wasn't a threat to you, either," I said bitterly. "He shouldn't be dead."

"His death was his own damn fault." Trek continued jabbing me with the gun, each stab causing new pain. "The kid should have known to run for cover the moment he heard gunshots."

"Only punks kill kids," Satch said, drawing Trek's anger away from me.

Trek smacked the shotgun against Satch's jaw. In the same instant, Rico swung his arm up, pushed his gun into the side of Trek's head, and pulled the trigger.

Anticipating the attack, Trek was already ducking. He pivoted beneath Rico's arm as the gun went off, the bullet discharging high. The silencer muffled the sound, but the shot was still loud, not like the soft *phut* heard in the movies. The bullet pierced the factory wall. Bricks and mortar burst out, leaving dust that billowed into the night before dissolving.

Trek stood upright and braced the butt of the shotgun against his hipbone, getting ready to fire. "Was that your way of volunteering for the bullet, Rico, or did you volunteer the day you stole the drugs I'd hidden behind the floorboard?"

My shoulders slumped.

"We all have to go some time," Rico said, then, looking up at the stars, he added with a grin, "It's a good night for dying."

I grabbed the end of the shotgun, surprising them both, and tilted it toward me, the metal warm compared to my icy fingers.

"I'm the one who talked them out of shooting Tony," I lied, hoping to turn Trek's anger away from Rico. "So if one of us has to die, it should be me." Then, willing to do anything to save Satch and Rico, I gave Trek a seductive smile. "Or, maybe, you and I can settle this another way."

"This is the way we're going to settle it," Trek said. "I'm going to send the bullet where it will give you the most pain."

Satch and Rico threw themselves at Trek as he ripped the shotgun from my hand and fired. A white flash exploded from the bore, scorching hot and blinding. My ears rang, aching from the blast.

Blood flooded my mouth, and more dripped down my chin. I slid my hand over the side of my blood-glazed face, searching for the entry wound, and found none. My breath came out in a wail. The blood seeping over my scalp and through my hair belonged to Rico, who lay on his back, blood pooling around his head.

Satch dropped to his knees and gripped Rico's hand, squeezing the corpse fingers, as if trying to keep Rico from slipping into death.

Trek walked away, not even glancing back.

A deep, primitive rage came over me. I took the hammer from my purse and ran after him, swung, and hit him, high between the shoulder blades.

He reeled around and thrust the gun hard into my solar plexus. Air escaped my lungs in an eerie whistle and I plunged to the ground. I could not move, could not catch my breath.

As I lay sprawled in the trash, Trek stepped closer and rested his foot on the side of my face, the sole of his shoe covered with mud that smelled of oil and decayed fish. "It's your fault, Blaise." Trek's voice penetrated the buzzing in my ears. "I was giving Rico a second chance. All he had to do was pull the trigger and shoot Tony's leg. He wouldn't be dead if you hadn't talked him and Satch out of doing what I'd sent the three of you out to do. Tony would have a busted kneecap, she might have even lost her leg, but Rico would be alive. So did you make the right choice?"

I shook my head, unable to speak.

Trek stared down at me, no emotion in his eyes. Satisfied, he lifted his foot and continued to the car, where Dante waited for him behind the steering wheel, the engine rumbling.

Quietly, the car drove off the lot and away, the whir of tires fading.

A heavy weight descended over me, squeezing my heart, cramping my lungs, suffocating me. I pulled myself up, and when I glanced down at Rico, the night shifted crazily, the ground moving out from under me.

30

The next thing I knew, I was lying behind a mound of trash, Satch beside me, his forehead covered with sweat. Through my daze, I became aware of voices shouting and cursing and screaming. A gunshot exploded, jarring me into full consciousness. I realized I had fainted.

Random shots, four in a row, hit trash bags less than six feet away. Whatever lay inside began to smolder. The acrid scent of burning plastic weaved into the air, carried on ringlets of smoke. I pressed my finger against my nose to stifle a sneeze.

Aware that I was conscious, Satch whispered, "Babo and his crew got here before I could carry you away. I only had time to hide us."

I turned onto my stomach and peered out at the Lobos. Two were spraying black paint over Rico's name, while three more fired guns, enraged by what Rico had done to their graffiti. A short distance away from them, Babo stood over the place where Rico had died.

"Why doesn't he see Rico?" I asked.

"I hid him while you were out. I didn't want Lobos to find his body."

I nodded my understanding as Babo looked up.

Something drew his attention back to the street. Immediately, he shouted, "*La chota, vatos,* run! *Andale!*"

The others lifted their heads, blue lights glinting over their faces, before they bolted from the lot and sprinted away, feet smacking the asphalt, their torn pant cuffs whipping behind their tennis shoes. At the crossroads, they split apart and ran in separate directions, as the *whoosh* of tires grew louder. Within seconds, two squad cars raced down the street, bar lights flashing though no sirens sounded.

"The gunshots finally pissed someone off enough to call the cops." Satch pulled himself up, then gave me his hand and helped me stand.

Concealing ourselves in shadows, wary of both police and Lobos, we set off for home.

Near Tulley's, we stole into a backyard and found a garden hose. Satch turned on the water and held the nozzle for me. I dunked my head under the flow and flinched from the cold, then scratched at the blood encrusted on my face, scraping it away until my skin felt raw and stung. My fingers were numb, my clothes sopping by the time I stepped back from the water.

Satch sprayed his face, then bent over, letting the stream gush over his head. His back hitched and, from his trembling, I knew he was crying and using the water to hide his tears. I pried the hose from his fingers and held it for him while he scrubbed. Minutes later, he wiped his hands over his eyes a final time and then turned off the water.

"Do you still have your father's gun?" he asked.

"You have lots of guns," I countered, tossing the hose aside. "Why do you need that one?"

"The cops confiscated the ones that belonged to my dad," Satch said as we started walking. "The only ones I have are the ones I bought myself, and street dealers don't sell reliable weapons to kids. I don't want to use something that's going to jam up when I face Trek."

"Do you want to end up in a hellhole prison like your dad?"

"Trek isn't done with us," Satch said. "The only way we're going to escape him is to kill him."

"Don't do anything until we've had a chance to think this through," I argued.

"There's no thinking to be done," Satch said. "Trek dies or we die. Nothing's going to change that."

"Promise me you'll wait," I said as we stopped next to my grandmother's garage. "Trek will expect us to retaliate tonight."

"We'll talk about it tomorrow, at school." He lifted the garage door, and as I started inside, he said, "Blaise."

I turned back and waited.

"After the cops arrested my dad, I ran away," he said softly. "I ran because they were going to put me in a foster home. I didn't want to live with strangers who would judge me by what my father had done. Rico kept me hidden in the Borderlands for five months until things got straightened out so my aunt could be my guardian."

Satch took a deep breath. "Rico and I were always there for each other. Some brothers aren't even that tight."

I understood what Satch was trying to tell me. He would probably never say the words to blame me for Rico's death. He didn't need to. I knew it was my fault. If I hadn't gotten in the way, trying to play the heroine, he and Rico could have taken Trek down, but because I had turned the gun until it was aimed at me, they had hesitated, and that pause had cost Rico his life.

Finally, he broke our silence. "No matter how you feel, you have to show up at school tomorrow and pretend like nothing's happened."

"Smile now, cry later," I said, repeating the gang girl's motto. "I'm good at pretending."

He let the garage door fall shut.

I pulled the house key from my purse and realized that I had left my hammer back at the vacant lot. I let myself inside and paused, leaning against the door, missing Rico, as my thumb automatically slid the dead bolt into place. With shock and disbelief settling over me, I crossed the kitchen. The moment I switched off the living room lamp, the music started, becoming louder until it resounded through the house. The front window shimmied with the thumping beat that came from the stolen Cadillac as it rolled to a stop in front of my grandmother's house.

Trek had been waiting for me to come home. He lifted the shotgun and aimed it at the front window. But I knew he wouldn't fire. He didn't believe in drive-bys. *You kill a guy and what then?* he had told me. *The guy's free of his sorry life. You got to terrorize your vic first. Let him feel death marching toward him.*

Trek had gotten the idea from watching a bullfight on TV. The fighting bull was butchered and eaten after the match. Its meat had a unique, bitter taste from the adrenaline released into its bloodstream during its fight with the matador. This had inspired Trek; he wanted his enemies to die with adrenaline flooding their veins the way it was pumping through mine now.

I stomped over to the door, flung it open and lunged outside, where I stood on the porch, daring him to shoot me, the wind cold against my still-wet body.

The shotgun came down and Trek smiled, then turned his gaze away from the house. The Cadillac rolled forward down the street, and soon the night songs of crickets and cicadas replaced the throbbing music from the SUV.

Trek had driven by to let me know that death was coming for me, but I refused to live my last days cowering.

31

The next morning, I awakened to the smells of bacon and coffee, my chest aching for Rico. My body felt too heavy to move, my grief an unbearable burden that pressed me down against the bed. I buried my face in my pillow so my grandmother wouldn't hear my cries.

"Blaise!" my grandmother yelled from downstairs. "You're going to be late if you don't hurry."

Slowly, I remembered Satch's warning that I had to go to school and pretend like nothing had happened. I forced myself out of bed, showered in steaming hot water, and put on my school uniform, then stole down the stairs and left before my grandmother could see my swollen eyes.

At the corner, Satch waited for me, the day already hot and sultry. He stared at the empty space between us, where Rico should have stood, and a terrible sigh escaped his chest, as if he had been holding in his sorrow, not wanting anyone but me to know how heartsick he felt.

His sadness seeped around me, heavier than the heat, and the urge to comfort him came over me. I pressed my hand against his side. Whether he was aware of my touch or not, I didn't know, but he didn't shrug me away either.

After a moment, he said, "I think I found an answer to our problem."

The flutter in my stomach told me I wasn't going to like his idea.

"Do you remember the Thanksgiving when I went to Colorado to see my dad?" he asked as we started walking.

"Of course."

The District didn't have a prison. Its convicted felons were sent to other states to serve out their terms. To visit his dad, Satch had flown to Colorado with his aunt. Afterward, when I had asked him about his visit, he'd acted like he hadn't heard my question.

"I gave my dad the story I'd written, the one that had won the school competition."

I nodded, remembering how proud Satch had felt.

"I put it in a binder along with the award. I couldn't give it to him face to face. We weren't allowed to touch or hug or anything like that. The guards gave it to him." Satch squinted up at the sky. A single drop of sweat rolled down his neck. He paused and used his shirttail to wipe his face. I tried not to stare at his tight stomach above the top of his low-slung jeans.

"My dad sat on the other side of this glass partition and kept thumbing through the pages," Satch said as we started forward again. "Every time he looked at me, he gave me this huge grin like he was really, finally proud of me."

"Wasn't he always?"

Satch set his hands on his hips. "Blaise, I'm trying to tell you something that I only told Rico before and if you interrupt me—"

"I'm sorry," I said quickly.

"I'd thought that maybe prison had changed him, because he didn't make fun of me for writing a story," Satch said.

"Why would he?" I asked.

"Because after my mom died, I wrote a poem, just something to get out my emotions. After my dad read it, he threw me to his homeboys and let them beat me into Core 9."

I didn't look at him. He and Rico had told me a different story about their jump-in.

"When I saw him the next day, he was furious. He said the guards must have stolen whatever I'd tried to give him inside the notebook, because he'd torn it apart and couldn't find a damn thing."

"I'm sorry," I whispered.

"So now, when I answer the phone and hear the recording that tells me the call is coming from a prison inmate, I hang up. I don't want my dad in my life." Satch paused. "But my dad can get us out of this situation with Trek. All I have to do is call him. I know the right words. The guards listening to the conversation won't understand what I'm saying, but my dad will. He'd jump at the chance to show me how powerful he still is."

I didn't like what I saw in Satch's eyes.

"What will your dad expect from you in return?" I asked as we reached school.

Ignoring my question, Satch said, "You'll never even know who the shooter is."

"Tell me what your dad will want," I demanded, my apprehension swelling.

"He'll want his son back," Satch chuckled grimly.

"Don't call him."

"Why not? I'm never going to make it out of here. You know I'm not. So why try? I'm not going to lie to myself anymore. The neighborhood won. It always wins. I'm a gangster. That's it."

"Don't even think about calling him. You can't."

"What's the alternative?" he asked in a harsh voice. "Do you think I can live like Dante, existing only to do Trek's bidding? I won't."

"I'm not suggesting that," I said. "I'll come up with a plan."

"A plan," he scoffed, turning away—then suddenly he turned back and clasped me against him, his lips on my forehead, breathing me in, the way Rico had done.

"What are you thinking?" I asked.

He opened his eyes and released me, then playfully nudged me up the school steps. "Hurry or we're going to be late for class. You don't want detention, do you? You'll have to sit with all those bad kids."

"Don't do anything," I warned.

"I'm not going to do a thing," he promised, his alacrity increasing my anxiety. "I'll wait for your plan."

We entered the hallway, where students shoved against each other, hiding drug deals, texting on cell phones, throwing gang signs and fists, while within the crowd, couples kissed and fondled each other, carried along to their classes in the stream of close bodies.

The 3Ts leaned against the wall near the staircase, their faces grim, eyes red and swollen like mine. Ariel had a wild look of disbelief and rage. Tanya said something to her and Ariel launched herself toward me, shouting my name.

Students stumbled and shifted to get out of her path; even so, she slugged her way toward me.

"Where's Rico?" she choked when she reached me.

"Why?" I hadn't been prepared for that question from anyone. My mind spun through all the ways she might have heard about his death. One name shot into my thoughts: *Trek*. Had he told the 3Ts what he had done? Then I saw Kaylee, standing by herself, her eyes swollen. Maybe she had been watching Trek's house late last night and had overheard him bragging to Omar about shooting Rico?

"I heard he was killed," Ariel said, her words quieting the students who stood near us. "He's dead, isn't he?"

"Who told you?" Satch asked, admitting the truth.

Ariel fell against him, gulping in air between her sobs.

Whispers spread through the crowd the way circles ripple out when a stone drops into deep water. Words like *dead, killed, Rico, gang* spilled from mouths that remained open in horror. Sorrow dampened the noise in the hallway and wreathed around us, not just for Rico, but for all of us; that we had to die so young and know funerals the way other kids knew proms. I felt sick and started toward the exit, no longer able to put up a false front.

As I rushed outside, the ringtone on my cell phone went off and Trek's number scrolled across the screen.

I lifted the phone to my ear. "What do you want?" I asked, my throat so tightened with anger, it hurt when I spoke.

"Hey, Blaise," Trek said, unaffected by my rage. "I don't believe in second chances, but if you and Satch give me what I want, then everything will be cool between us. I think you've learned your lesson."

My heart picked up a faster beat, detecting Trek's lie. He was never going to give us a second chance.

"This is the way I like you, not talking back," Trek said when I didn't speak. "I'll see you tonight."

He hung up.

I tried to think calmly. Trek expected to see Satch and me after school so he could tell us how he wanted us to deal with Tony. If we refused to shoot her, he would kill Satch. I had no doubt that he would. And even if we did shoot Tony and Trek did give us a second chance, everyone would eventually find out that Trek had killed Rico, our best friend, and that we had done nothing. Respect. Honor. Reputation. We would lose all three and, without those, we were nothing.

The ground swayed as frightening ideas continued to stir inside me. I didn't want to give my grandmother more pain. She'd be destroyed if I were arrested for murder, but sometimes the right choice caused suffering for the people we loved. And that was never a good reason to back down from doing what was morally right.

Morally right? A shudder raced through me. *How could murder ever be right?*

The wind stopped and the stillness that followed seemed unnatural, oppressive even and, in that instant, I knew that the irresistible forces of fate had been pulling me forward to this moment, in which I had to decide the impossible.

If I killed Trek—*Please, God, strike me dead, first*—Omar or Dante would kill me before I could get away. If I didn't kill Trek, then he would kill Satch tonight, and his death, which would be my fault because I had not killed Trek, would leave me so deadened that I would welcome the bullets when Trek killed me, his last witness. Either way, my life ended, but with the first choice, though I died, Satch lived.

Maybe my destiny had always been to sacrifice myself so Satch could live and thrive and escape the neighborhood. That was noble, heroic even, to give up everything for a friend. Most people were willing to die to save someone they loved, but how many were willing to kill so their loved one could live free?

My father had purchased the six-inch-barrel Smith & Wesson .357 magnum revolver because it could endure long periods of neglect and still function. At the time, the reasoning behind his choice had seemed odd. Now I wondered if he had had an inkling of premonition that I would one day need a gun. Had he felt a tremor of uneasiness, as I did now, when he'd touched the trigger? Maybe, at times, the future did send enough energy back to influence our decisions in the present.

I slid the gun into the back of my waistband, then adjusted my T-shirt and brushed my hand over the bulge. It didn't feel too noticeable. Still, any gangster would know I was armed, but I was counting on everyone being inside because of the heat.

Before I left, I looked in on my grandmother, curled under her covers, the oscillating fan blasting artificial wind about her room. I stepped over to her bed and kneeled beside her.

She stirred as I started to kiss her good-bye.

"What's wrong, baby?" she asked drowsily, more asleep than awake.

"Nothing," I said, my voice thin with the need to cry.

She petted my face, her fingers cold. I took her hand, the swollen knuckles protruding against my palm, and whispered, "I love you."

"I love you, too," she said, her eyes closing.

I kissed her forehead, then tucked her hand beneath the covers and left.

Outside, no one sat on their stoops, and even little kids had deserted their plastic wading pools for the cooler air inside. I passed the park, the hot sunlight wilting the newly seeded grass, and ducked behind a hedge to stake out Trek's house and see what I had to go up against.

Across the street, without any comfort of shade, Omar lazed on a lawn chair, drinking beer, a pyramid of crushed cans in front of him. Because the weather had not driven him inside, I assumed he was on guard while Trek slept in his bedroom.

I studied the house, mentally planning my escape. I had never been on the second floor, but if Omar blocked my getaway down the stairs, then I could climb out the front upstairs windows and jump to the ground from the porch roof. Satisfied, I snuck back the way I had come and headed for the alley, fear slithering into my belly.

Trek depended on Bonnie and Pixie to guard the back entrance, but neither dog growled when I pushed through the gate. They stayed in the shade of a bay tree, near their water bowl. Bonnie rolled over and offered me her belly as if in apology for not bouncing on her feet to greet me. Pixie, languishing in the heat, only blinked.

I tested the doorknob and left an imprint from my clammy skin. I had hoped to find the door unlocked. Now I had to locate the key. Kaylee knew its hiding place and, though she hadn't told me where, the ragged doormat triggered a memory.

In eighth grade, I had been impressed with Kaylee's cleverness when she'd cut a pocket into the back of her doormat to hide her key. Now, I wondered if the idea had been hers. I lifted Trek's mat, the wiry fibers prickling my fingers, and found a slit on the backside that was scaled with dirt. I wiggled my finger inside, pinched out a key, and used it to let myself onto the porch.

My confidence unraveled when I stepped into the kitchen and found the door to the dining room closed. Trek only shut it when important business was going on in another part of the house. Maybe a congregation of gangsters sat in the living room, and Omar was watching the street as a lookout in case police cars sped around the corner.

I listened, my legs trembling, and tried to determine who might be in the next room. The silence told me nothing. I squeezed the doorknob, turning it until the latch clicked, then waited.

When no one came to investigate, I stole into the dining room and, after carefully closing the door behind me, took out my gun. Its heavy weight emboldened me.

I inched toward the living room, where weapons sat on the coffee table, next to an ashtray filled with cigarette butts, some still smoldering and weaving smoke into the humid air. How many gangsters were in there? I heard no voices, only muffled rumblings.

Careful to lead with the gun, I peered around the corner.

Dante sat alone, in a gaming chair with force feedback that vibrated when explosions flashed across the TV screen. Ash fell from the cigarette clenched between his teeth as his thumbs hit the control. On the TV screen, more blasts destroyed the video-game landscape, the volume so high, the booms leaked from his headphones. In the cyber-drama, Dante was playing the good guy, a hero rescuing hostages from gangsters like us.

Though a gun rested between his bare feet, he wasn't a threat. His breath reeked of alcohol, the rank smell saturating the room. If he tried to fire, he'd stumble and shoot the wall.

My heart racing, I snuck behind him and started up the stairs. By the time I reached the fifth step, the wind chimes that dangled from the railing began swirling overhead, seashells lazily tinging against metal tubes, their movement setting other chimes pinging into motion. I froze, suddenly aware that this was another safeguard to protect Trek while he slept, the noise an alarm to awaken him if an intruder got past his bodyguards and prowled up the stairs. I listened for footsteps, the movement of someone going for a gun, but the only sounds came from the drowsy jingling above me.

My eyes flicked down to the living room and back to the hallway above me, trying to cover every direction from which an ambush might come. At the same time, my thoughts jumped back to the door leading into the dining room. It should have been open. Closed, it prevented a draft from flowing through the house and starting the chimes if someone broke through the back door. Trek would have left it open while he slept, so maybe he wasn't even home.

I took the next step in slow motion, sweat trickling down my back, and decided that if Trek wasn't in his bed, then I would wait for him there, curled against his pillows. I had almost reached the landing when the back door opened. I stood exposed and trapped, unable to run either way without rousing the wind chimes. I braced myself against the wall, prepared to fire, my wrists aching from the weight of the gun, as my heart trilled its beats.

From the kitchen came the sound of the refrigerator opening. Bottles clanked and cans screaked over the metal racks. Then the refrigerator door closed, the footsteps retreated, and the person left the house.

In the same moment, I knew Trek was home. Omar had closed the door to the dining room so he could come and go and get his cold beer, without setting off the seashells and glass chimes and awakening Trek. By doing so, he had unwittingly left Trek vulnerable. I smiled at his stupidity.

Drink up, I thought. The drunker he became, the better my chances of living, and I wanted to live, not just for my selfish self, but for my grandmother, who had already grieved enough.

I reached the landing and faced three open doors that led off the hallway. After finding no one in the first two rooms, I crept to the front bedroom, where the windows were open, though no breeze stirred the hot air. Someone was sleeping on the bed, under the silken black sheet, a gun on the nightstand. I was tempted to shoot and run, but I couldn't fire blindly. I had to lift the covers and see Trek's face to know I had the right target.

A yawn alerted me to movement on the bed. I tightened my

grip on the gun, my fingers slippery with sweat, and eased against the wall. What I had thought had been the contour of one person underneath the covers split into two. Seconds later, Melissa lifted the sheet off her head and stood.

I slipped into an open closet and, through the crack between the door and frame, caught a glimpse of more finger-grip bruises on her arm.

The murmur of wind chimes rose and fell, following her down the hallway. A door closed and, shortly after, the sound of running water filled the stillness. I assumed she was taking a shower. That gave me minutes before she returned.

I stepped out from my hiding place and stopped cold.

Trek was sitting up in bed, staring at me, his pitch-black eyes revealing no surprise. "You look gorgeous when you're terrified," he said.

Adrenaline buzzed through me, igniting my courage. I held the gun higher and circled around the bed for a better aim. The first shot had to hit him, because as soon as I fired, Trek would lunge for the gun on the nightstand.

"You should have shot me while I was sleeping," he said, his grin too confident. "Now you've got yourself in a dicey situation."

His gaze flitted behind me before settling back, his eyes gleaming with enjoyment. Was someone creeping up behind me? Melissa? Had the shower been a ruse? I didn't dare look with Trek's hand so close to the nightstand gun.

I aimed at his chest, anticipating the blast, my arms and wrists ready for the recoil.

"You can't do it," Trek said. "You're just one of my herd. No guts. No brains. Nothing but a beautiful body."

I pulled the trigger.

Click.

The gun misfired. My heart surged, swelling my temples with the ferocity of its beats.

Triumph flashed in Trek's eyes. He lunged across the bed, grabbed the gun off the nightstand and swung around, his grin huge.

Knowing that I was about to die, an eerie calm came over me. My father had told me that if I ever got a dud round, or a misfire, I needed to fire again to rotate the cylinder. With no time to take a stance and prepare myself, I squeezed the trigger as Trek raised his gun and aimed at me.

My bullet discharged. The power from the blast ripped through my arms and, unable to control the strength of the recoil, my hands flew back, and the gun slammed into my forehead. Pain spun through my skull as the roar of the shot echoed about the room.

Trek slumped over, blood pouring from his head onto the pillow.

I blinked back tears, terrified by what I had done, and averted my eyes so I would not see death on Trek's face.

Inside the ringing in my ears came the sounds of Melissa screaming, the dogs barking, and Omar barging through the front door, starting the wind chimes into clattering motion.

"Why the hell did you fire the gun?" he yelled at Dante, and though I couldn't hear Dante's reply, I heard Omar ask, "If you didn't fire, then who did?"

A moment later, Omar shouted, "Trek?"

I staggered to the window and, using the gun like a hammer, knocked out the screen. The frame skittered across the porch roof and fell to the lawn. From this angle, the jump looked much higher than it had when I had studied it from below, and my body, still shaken, wrists and elbows weak from the recoil, wouldn't be able to jump with my normal agility. I'd break an ankle, maybe both legs.

Footsteps pounded up the stairs, the raucous noise from the wind chimes warning me that I had only seconds before Omar stormed into the room. I hid in the closet, blood trickling into my eyes, and held the gun at my side. I refused to fire again, even in self-defense, and waited for the bullets to take me.

Omar stomped into the room, his steps thunderous and huge. He stopped and sucked in air that he exhaled in curses. Dante's bare feet padded in after him, the smoke from his cigarette engulfing the smells of Omar's beer breath and sweat.

"The shooter used the window!" Omar shouted. "Get the car. We can still catch him."

They charged from the room, the wind chimes jangling, as they stampeded down the stairs. Their beer-soaked minds hadn't considered that the killer might still be inside.

Moments later, the Pontiac started. The engine knocked and sputtered, but the car didn't speed away as I had anticipated. The driver kept gunning the engine until exhaust seeped in through the window, a gray haze sagging into the hot room. The longer the car idled, the more convinced I became that Omar and Dante had realized their blunder and that one of them was coming back to search for the killer inside the house.

I needed to leave, but first I had to find out what they were doing. I crept over to the window, the dull ache in my head intensifying when I peered out into the afternoon glare.

Dante stood next to the Pontiac, looking nervous and squinting at Omar, who pointed back at the house. From the way Dante was nodding, I guessed that Omar was giving him instructions.

I glanced down the hallway. Crying in the bathroom, Melissa must have understood that Trek had been killed. Eventually she was going to come out and call for help. Omar had most likely realized this, too, and was giving Dante the task of hiding the guns. They couldn't risk having the coroner and the police come into the house with so many weapons brazenly displayed in the living room.

The moment Dante started toward the front door, I left the room, without once glancing at Trek, and loped down the hallway.

From behind the bathroom door, Melissa whimpered, "I didn't do it. You have to believe me."

The desperation in her voice stopped me. Reflexively, I grabbed the doorknob, wanting to comfort her, and almost called her name before caution overruled me. I turned away and plunged down the stairs, taking them two at a time.

The heat thickened near the Anacostia River, the air infested with stinkbugs and flies that landed on my face as I plodded through trash in the vacant lot. The Lobos had sprayed new graffiti over the factory wall, but the gold-painted *RICO* still bled through their colors, the letters shimmering in the sunlight.

I stopped where Rico had died and dropped my father's gun on the bloodstained earth, my body feverish with hate. I could have killed Trek all over again for what he'd done to Rico, Melissa, and Kaylee.

Wiping the tears off my cheeks, I wondered how I was still alive. Once I had stolen inside Trek's house, I had thought of myself as dead and, though I had planned an escape, I had never believed that I could make it out. Yet, here I was, tempting fate to end my life with bullets from a Lobos patrol.

By the time the moon had risen behind the misty clouds and no one had shot me, I knew that fate was protecting me because it still had plans for me. I wondered what dreadful purpose I had left to serve as I walked home through the Lobos' neighborhood without my usual caution. I didn't stop until I stood in front of my grandmother's scraggy roses, which had to skimp and wait for rain because our water bill was too high. The blossoms drooped, their petals spiraling to the ground. I caught a handful and, breathing their sweetness, trudged inside and up the stairs, ignoring the light my grandmother had left on for me.

In the bathroom, I took off my clothes, stuffed them into the hamper, and stepped into the drizzling shower. Goose bumps broke across my body. The water heater had gone out again. I dried off and then studied the wound on my forehead in the mirror.

Blood oozed from the gash, the skin distended and warm, infection already festering in the swelling that was tender to my touch. I grabbed the scissors to cut my hair and paused. Even thicker bangs couldn't hide the mark that revealed what I had done.

I stared at the solemn girl in my reflection.

"You're not who I am," I whispered, as if my face belonged to a stranger. "You're what the neighborhood has made me, but you're not me."

The odd feeling that my reflection was detached, a separate and alive mystical twin, stopped as if I had suddenly awakened. I had never heard of anyone falling asleep while standing, eyes wide open, but I supposed I could have dozed off; the sensation had been that of a dream. Even so, while I pulled on my sweats, I kept glancing back at the mirror, half-expecting my doppelganger to peer out at me.

I hurried to my room and grabbed my cell phone, stunned to discover I had no messages. No one had even tried to call. Alarm twitched through me. I rubbed my fingers against my breastbone, trying to calm myself.

I supposed that Trek's death wasn't the kind of news that was left in a message. Maybe the 3Ts or Kaylee or Ariel were watching the house, waiting for me to come home. I hadn't turned off the living room light, so how would they know I was here? I raced downstairs, switched off the lamp, and listened, expecting footsteps to pound up the porch steps.

The only sound came from distant music, which grew louder until the *boom-boom-boom-bah* shuddered the walls. I fell to the floor, my will to live surprising me, and crawled to the window, expecting to see gun barrels pointed at the house.

A blue Buick parked at the curb, Dante behind the steering wheel. The music stopped and Satch jumped out. I scrambled to the door and opened it before Satch could knock, then stepped back, letting darkness swallow me.

"Trek's been shot," Satch announced as he stepped inside, his gaze settling on the shadow where I stood. "The bullet cut a path over his scalp, skinned right through his hair."

My heart pounded a paroxysm of beats. If Trek was alive, why hadn't he told Satch that I shot him? Or had he?

"Omar got drunk and let the shooter get inside," Satch said. "Trek's fired him and he's mad as hell because, afterward, Omar was so wild for revenge that he didn't even check to see if Trek was still alive. He left him for dead. Melissa and Dante took Trek to the hospital, but he could have bled to death. We're going there now to pick him up. Come on with us."

"So Trek's your friend again?" I said accusingly. "You told

me there was no way around it, either Trek dies or we die, but obviously you found another way."

"Don't you understand?" Satch said, easing closer. "Trek's going to be maniacal about catching whoever shot him. He won't have time for anything else."

"So you think he's going to forget that we're witnesses—"

"—of course not—"

"—and not come after us?"

"This just gives us time to get him," Satch said.

"How long?"

"We won't know until we see him. Let's go. Dante's waiting."

"And why are you with Dante?"

"He's a ride, nothing more. Trek's going to dump him, too. Melissa said that Dante got as drunk as Omar." Satch offered me his hand. "Don't you want to see Trek and gloat? No one's ever gotten to him before."

"Are you the lure, Satch?" I asked, the heaviness in my heart unbearable. "Are you supposed to convince me that it's safe to get into the car with you and Dante?"

"What?"

I stepped into the light so he could see my forehead.

He flinched. "You should have waited for me." His anger sounded sincere, but a good lure had to be a good actor, too. "You can't go out to the car. Dante knows what that mark means and, more than anything right now, he wants to redeem himself in Trek's eyes. He'll call Trek and tell him you're the shooter."

"Trek knows who shot him," I said calmly. "He watched me pull the trigger."

"The bullet gave him a concussion, so maybe he can't remember." Satch spoke so earnestly that I almost believed him.

"Trek could be lying to you," I suggested, watching Satch's response. "Lots of people lie when it's to their advantage." I stepped away from Satch, my hand gliding over my grandmother's wedding picture, willing to throw it at him if he came at me.

"The attic," he said suddenly. "Escape through the attic."

"And what will you tell Dante when you go back to the car without me?" I asked, my suspicion mounting.

"I'll say you wanted to change your clothes. That'll give you time to get away."

I didn't move. The emptiness inside me felt odd; the stillness, the quiet. After all my rage and terror, I felt nothing. Perhaps I had had too many emotions, more than my heart could handle, and as a safety precaution, my mental circuit breaker had shut down all feeling.

"Go!" Satch stepped back, giving me room to race past him. "Hurry! Before Dante decides to come inside to see what's taking so long."

I only had one way to find out if I could trust Satch. I raced up the stairs to the second floor landing, grabbed the rope connected to the folding ladder in the attic, and yanked hard. The ladder clattered down and, before it had even settled, I jumped onto the bottom rung and scurried up, my speed an act for Satch.

Breathing the dust and heat stored from the day, I balanced on the top rung. When the front door closed, I climbed down, shoved the ladder into place, and made my way to the living room window.

The Buick was no longer in front. I hadn't expected it to be. Dante had driven down the street to Satch's house, where it was less risky for Satch to grab me.

Satch hadn't been able to entice me out to the car and, if he'd tried to force me, I would have fought him. Then, when my grandmother found her living room in shambles and me missing, she would have called the police, who would have investigated my disappearance as a crime. In his own home, Satch could clear away any evidence of my struggle and, after, everyone would believe my disappearance was simply that of another runaway.

I couldn't blame Satch for betraying me. To survive he had to prove that he was down for Trek, and turning against me proved that more than shooting Tony.

He and Dante were probably laughing, anticipating the shock and fear on my face when I descended from the attic into Satch's hallway. Once they realized I had outmaneuvered them, they'd come back, lusting for revenge.

I left through the back door, caught in the gangster's dilemma. I needed to call the cops and ask them to protect me, but I couldn't call them because I'd committed too many crimes of my own. I headed toward the wasteland of vacant buildings to the window where I usually broke in, but since my last visit, the District had switched from plywood for boarding up the windows to steel screens. When I tried to pry the screen loose, the sharp edges sliced my skin. I left the frame slippery with blood and considered my options. I'd have to hide out in the garages near Tulley's.

I had almost reached the street when the call tone from a cell phone broke the stillness. I dropped to the ground and slid under a wisteria, the purple flowers fluttering their fragrance around me.

While Dante talked on the phone, Satch, who lagged behind him, bent down to examine what Dante had ignored, my footprints in the fallen wisteria petals.

My fingers closed around the neck of a discarded bottle. Though I could release my feral instincts on Dante and jam the glass into his eye, I didn't know if I could attack Satch with the same ferocity.

Dante ambled back to Satch, pulling his attention away from the petals, and handed him the phone. "Trek wants to talk to you."

Speaking loudly, as if Trek was groggy from painkillers, Satch said into the phone, "We'll find her. She'll try the vacant buildings first, and then the garages near Tulley's. I know all her hiding spots."

I thought of a place that Satch might not know. Years before I had even been born, my grandfather had built a box against the house to cover the gas meter. A new electronic model had replaced the old meter, but the little shed still housed the original, which my grandmother had called an eyesore. I might be able to hide inside.

After Satch and Dante turned the corner, I slipped away and ran quietly to my house.

Less than waist high, the shed seemed too small. Rust and dirt flaked off the bolt as I worked it loose and lifted the latch. The door wobbled open, the hinges rattling nervously as I squeezed into the cobwebs filled with insect husks, and curled over the meter and pipes, my back pressed against the top planks. I pinched a cross board and pulled the door closed.

Within minutes, my feet started to go numb. I had crammed myself in so tightly that I was never going to be able to spring out and run if they found me.

Dante's laughter rang out from somewhere near. He didn't even have enough sense to be stealthy when they stalked me. I wondered why Satch wasn't warning him to be quiet.

Silence followed. I tensed, my calves and thighs quivering. What were they doing? If they had gone past my house, I should have heard their steps. My heart sank. I knew they had found me even before the cross board snapped from my fingers and the door swung open.

Satch stood, staring down at me.

"Nothing but an old gas meter and cobwebs," Satch lied, slamming the door before Dante could see me. "A little kid couldn't even fit inside. I don't know why you wanted to check it."

A click of metal told me Satch had closed the latch, but when the deadbolt rasped into the slot, the hope that he had been protecting me evaporated. He had no reason to lock me inside unless he planned to keep me trapped so he could take me to Trek himself.

"You didn't let me see," Dante complained, his shadow flickering over the light that came through the cracks.

"Why do you need to?" Satch asked. "I already looked."

"Trek asked me to find her," Dante argued, but his tone conveyed that he was backing down.

"We better check the garages near Tulley's," Satch said, stepping away. "That's where she'll be."

"All right," Dante agreed too readily.

I knew he was going to come back, alone, the moment he could. He had a dangerous need to please Trek and was clearly suspicious.

As soon as the only sound came from the stuttering swamp cooler across the street, I pressed my foot against the door and bore down, trying to bust the hinges. Nothing gave way. After my second attempt failed, I squirmed off the meter and shoved my shoulder and head against the door.

The hinges jangled and nails creaked, pulling from the wood. A board cracked with a loud snap and the shed shifted. I lost my balance and slipped down, caught between the meter and the bolted door. I could barely breathe.

I edged my foot flat against the rear of the shed, then pushed off the back wall, using the strength of my leg to ram my body against the door. Blood rushed to my temples. I knew I couldn't last much longer. With all my remaining energy, I gave a final shove.

Wood rasped with an eerie screech. The door split open and I fell onto the grass as the shed broke apart, an explosion of wood. A board hit the bridge of my nose, and then I lay still, gulping air, letting the pain hold me as the cramps in my muscles loosened. The effort had left me drained and shaking.

Slowly, I became aware of the *boom-boom-boom-bah* of music. Dante was returning sooner than I had thought possible. I rolled onto my belly, splinters impaling my skin, and dragged myself off the shattered wood. Blood dripped from my nose, pattering onto the grass, as I crawled toward the porch. The space under the stoop, where my grandmother stored her gardening tools, offered me refuge. I wriggled in and grabbed the hand cultivator. The claw, used to weed the soil, made a lethal weapon.

The Buick pulled up to the curb, the music died, and Dante,

alone in the car, stared at the broken shed, his face confused, his last hope stolen. I almost felt a twinge of pity for him. He wanted so desperately to belong, but respect was hard won and easily lost, and Dante had lost his. He had backed down too many times, proving he no longer had the fearlessness needed to be a Core 9 gangster. He drove away, the music silent, defeat in his slow speed.

Unlike Dante, Satch would understand that I had injured myself. I needed to leave before he returned. A gardening tool wouldn't be enough to stop him.

As I staggered across the street, muffled *thumping* came from down the block. With only seconds to hide, I threw myself beneath my neighbor's swamp cooler, where shadows covered me. The muddy water from the constant dripping soaked into my sweats and eased the sting of the splinters in my arms.

From behind a cluster of bobbing dandelions, I watched Ariel and the 3Ts run up to my house, men's wool socks pulled over their tennis shoes to hush the clap of their soles on the pavement. Ariel used the key that I had given her to unlock the door and they vanished inside.

I tried to ignore the ache in my chest that prompted my annoying need to cry. A shooting within a gang always forced its members to reconsider their loyalties. Those were the consequences of taking a stand, nothing worth crying over. Even so, I hadn't expected Ariel or the 3Ts to turn against me.

A light came on in my bedroom, a half circle over the wall. For some reason, they had set my desk lamp on the floor. When a car turned the corner, the bedroom light went out and four figures appeared at my window. As they watched the car, I wondered if they thought I had defected and shot Trek for money, paid by an enemy gang.

After the car passed, they stepped away from the window and the light switched on, again. I settled back in the mud and, wincing from the pain, began to flex my ankles, pulling against the knots in my thighs and calves. Though Ariel and I had wrestled against each other, the 3Ts had never fought me. At the jump-in, I hadn't been allowed to fight back. This time I could, and they would feel the difference.

Hours later, the front door opened. Ariel and the 3Ts snuck down the porch steps, leaving my house as furtively as they had come. I scanned the misty morning, certain Trek would send someone else to watch my house, and when I saw no one, I dashed across the street. I slipped inside, grabbed my cell phone off the coffee table, and listened to my only message as I raced up the stairs and shut myself in the bathroom.

"Blaise," Trek's groggy voice said. "Call me. We've got things to discuss."

I hated his smugness and texted back two words before I stepped into the shower and let the cold spray wash over my swollen nose, knowing that if my grandmother came home, she would think I was getting ready for school, unaware that this was the last time she would see me. A cry sputtered from my lips when I thought of her, but I choked back the sob and steeled myself. I didn't have time to cry.

In my bedroom, my hair dripping water down my back,

I rushed into my closet and looked through the hand-me-downs that I never wore. I dressed in jeans, a purple paisley blouse, a pink sweater, and the shoes that the 3Ts had bought me. Quickly, I packed a nightgown, underwear, and a wide-brimmed, floppy hat into my purse, then slid my phone into my pocket.

As I hurried to leave, I glanced down and stopped. On the floor, tucked under my lamp, was a stack of money. I felt overwhelmed. My friends hadn't abandoned me, after all. They had left an unopened pack of cigarettes with the money, though I didn't smoke, to let me know they had given me everything they had and were wishing me well.

I picked up the money and the cigarettes and stuffed them into my purse as a car pulled up outside. I glanced out my bedroom window. A police officer was climbing out of a squad car, undoing the snap on his gun holster. Blood drained from my head. Had Trek given me up to the cops?

Anxiety tripped me up, but only for seconds. I still had time to escape through the back. I rushed down the stairs and almost collided into my grandmother, who was crossing the living room.

Fear came to her eyes the moment she saw the mark on my forehead. "God have Mercy, what did you do?" She clenched me in her bony arms, the scents of Pine-Sol and Clorox wafting off her.

"Your life will be better without me," I said, prying myself from her embrace.

"You are my life," she replied, her voice frail and desperate.

A terrible hollowness spread through me. "I'm sorry," I said before I dashed into the kitchen.

As I started to open the back door, heavy pounding came from the other side. "Police!"

A second officer had come through the alley. I raced back the way I had come, past my grandmother, and up the stairs.

"Lord Jesus," my grandmother moaned, not answering either door, though knocking on both drummed through the house. She collapsed on the steps behind me, falling into prayer, beseeching Jesus to enter my heart and guide me.

In the upstairs hallway, I caught the rope to the trap door and tugged the ladder down, then scaled the rungs to the attic, where I pulled the ladder up after me. I locked it in place and darted off, zigzagging around dusty boxes to the wall where Satch's father had hammered a hole. With plaster and broken laths scrunching under my feet, I scurried into our neighbor's attic. The smells of breakfast changed as I stumbled through three more.

At last, I balanced on the ladder above Satch's home and gave a slight jump. The ladder descended faster than I had anticipated, falling out from under me. I leaped to the floor and crashed against the wall, the ladder banging down at the same time. I listened to the silence that followed, hoping no one was home.

"Blaise," Satch's voice came from behind me.

I spun around.

On the other side of the ladder, Satch stood in his briefs, blinking as if the noise had startled him awake, his beautiful, muscled body blocking my way to the stairs.

"I'm glad you got away last night," he said too quickly.

Bitter resentment tightened my chest. I edged forward, swinging my purse, wishing I still had my hammer, and paused.

"I believed Trek last night when he said he didn't know who shot him," Satch said. "I swear I didn't know you were the shooter."

I wondered if he could see the doubt in my eyes, the anger, as I eased around the ladder, closer to the stairs.

"Please believe me, Blaise. Trek was the one who told Dante about the escape route through the attic, not me."

"So what? You didn't stop him from driving down to your house, did you?" I glanced over the banister at the stairs. If I tried to jump, I'd probably break my neck.

"You know I saw you," Satch continued, still trying to dispel my distrust. "I spoke loud enough for you to hear me. I wanted you to get away."

"You locked me in the shed," I blurted. "So you could take me to Trek yourself."

"Come on, Blaise. The door was rickety. It would have swung open the moment I let go and Dante would have seen you. I've been protecting you."

"Like hell." I plunged forward and swung my purse at his crotch. He jumped back, dodging my hit, then bounded forward and caught me before my foot hit the top step. He trapped me in his arms, forcing me to face him, his eyes intense with anger.

I shoved against him, trying to break free, but he only tightened his grip. "I love you, Blaise."

I stopped struggling and looked up at his enticing smile, those captivating eyes that held me transfixed.

"You're so good at charming girls," I rasped. "You're just amazing. You knew the exact words to say to make me stop fighting, but you should know those words hurt when they're a lie."

"It's not a lie. I couldn't tell you before because Rico was already in love with you, and no way could I disrespect him by going after you, not after all the things he'd done for me. All our lives Rico and I only had each other to count on. That's why I tried to keep away from you."

I searched his eyes. The sincerity in them gave me hope.

"That night in your garage after Trek shot Rico, I was trying to tell you, but I couldn't bring myself to say the words with Rico just killed."

Sadness flowed through me. "Did Rico know how you felt?"

"Of course he did. We never kept anything from each other."

Finally, I understood why Rico was afraid I would hate him for being selfish. He had watched me falling in love with Satch and hadn't stepped aside so that we could be together. But I couldn't hate Rico, not for loving me so deeply.

I smoothed my hands over Satch's chest, relishing his warm skin. As he leaned down to kiss me, a sudden worry shot through me. "Is Trek after you?" I asked.

"No," Satch said, lazily stroking my back, his breath mingling with mine. "He believed me when I told him that I'd trapped you inside the shed so I could take you to him myself."

"Are you sure?"

"Relax, Blaise," Satch whispered. "I can handle my own."

The pleasant ache that I remembered from before stirred

252

inside me. This hadn't been part of my plan and, though I knew I should run, my feelings for Satch were making me careless.

As he led me into his bedroom, his cell phone sounded. He ignored it and pressed me against him.

I startled when his lips finally touched mine. Breathless, I clasped his back, pulling him closer, my heart quickening.

I was about to force myself to pull away when his cell phone pinged again. Annoyed, Satch grabbed it from his nightstand, glanced at the screen, and froze. "What?" I asked.

"Trek's at the front door."

"I'll handle this." Satch pulled on his jeans and rushed headlong into the hallway.

When I grabbed my purse and raced after him, he wheeled around, his voice low and angry. "Do you still think I'm going to hand you over to Trek?"

I shook my head.

"Then prove to me that you trust me by waiting here."

"I can't," I said, panic setting in as I realized how incautious I had been. "I have to leave. Cops are down at my house."

Astonishment and disbelief flashed over his face before he brought his emotions under control. "You're as crazy as Rico. Why'd you let me kiss you?"

"For the memory," I whispered. "I'm running away."

"You can't. Too many girls from our neighborhood have tried and they always end up dead."

"I don't have a choice," I said.

Looking crazed with sorrow, Satch pressed his lips against my forehead, and then abruptly pulled back and touched the side of my face, his gaze lingering, as if he was trying to get a picture of me to hold in his heart.

"I'll give you cover," he said, his expression hardening, before he charged down the stairs.

When I heard the front door open, I eased onto the landing. Though I couldn't hear their conversation, Satch nodded in agreement to whatever Trek was saying and stepped out on the porch, closing the door behind him.

With quick, jittery steps, I hurried down to the living room. In the kitchen, I broke into a run, slammed out the back door, and dashed into the alley. I glanced over my shoulder at the police car still parked behind my grandmother's home, then darted onto the street.

The bus had stopped and people were boarding. I shoved into the line, jumped on, and paid my fare. As the bus pulled away from the curb, I stared straight ahead and let my silent tears fall.

Near Gallery Plaza, I got off the bus and rode the escalator down into the Metro station. The moldering smells in the entrance tunnel filled my lungs as I stepped into the dingy light and inserted an old ticket into the slot. I looked up to where the security cameras recorded me, certain I appeared distraught, a terrified girl on the run.

I rode the second escalator down to the platform and let the crowd pull me to the safety line, where I stood amid the red flashing floor lights.

The train stopped and passengers mobbed around me, coming

and going, their bodies hiding me from the cameras. I took the hat from my purse, set it on my head, the floppy brim covering my eyes, then yanked off the pink sweater and swaddled it around my purse, which I cradled in my arms.

As the crowd thinned, I walked away, pretending to be a young mother leaving the Metro Station, carrying her baby and grinning wildly. My grandmother and Satch were telling everyone that I had run away, but I had no intention of leaving. I wasn't going to let Trek destroy more lives. He was a dead man.

36

I hid in Chinatown, sunlight streaking into the alley, where I sat on a crate of bok choy while sipping coffee that I had purchased inside the restaurant. I should have tossed my cell phone, but even with the risk that the police could use it to track me, I kept it clutched in my hand, anxious to hear from Satch. I couldn't risk calling him, because I feared Trek would be watching him closely. Satch had taken a terrible risk to protect me, and I wasn't as convinced as he was that Trek had believed him.

By nightfall, I could no longer control the impulse to go to Satch's house and find out if he was all right. Though I had planned to wait until the streets emptied, I stood and, walking into the winds of an approaching storm, headed home.

As I neared my neighborhood, lightning crackled across the sky. The streetlights flared, then dimmed to an orange filament glow before brightening again. Seconds later, thunder rocked the night and, when the rumbling quieted, the downpour began. Rain spattered the ground, releasing the lush scents of wet earth and grass.

Within the barrage of pattering rain, I became aware that my phone was sounding. The caller ID read "Satch." Relief flooded through me. I answered without thinking. "Satch, are you all right?"

"That's an odd way to answer the phone." Trek's voice came over the connection. "Why are you worried about Satch when he was part of the posse that was hunting for you?"

I froze, my stomach sick with panic.

When I didn't say anything, Trek added, "If Satch had turned on me, I'd want him dead, five bullets in his head."

The words twisted into me, bringing forth the memory of how easily Trek had killed Rico. I slumped against the nearest car, an old Ford with deflated tires. Did Trek know that Satch had deceived him?

"I got Satch," Trek answered as if I had spoken the question aloud. "But you're the one I want."

"I'll trade," I said, grateful that Satch wasn't dead.

"Where are you?" Trek asked.

"An hour from the neighborhood," I lied, listening. I could hear wind chimes in the background, which meant Trek was standing near the stairs in his house. Hope raced through me. If Satch was hostage in one of the rooms, then maybe I could free him without a trade.

"I'll come get you," Trek offered, interrupting my thoughts.

"I'm at Dulles," I embroidered my lie as lightning raced across the clouds and split into jagged seams. Simultaneously, thunder shattered the night, rocking the ground. The electricity went out.

"Dulles?" Trek laughed. "Are you catching a plane?"

"I'll meet you near Tulley's in an hour." I ended the conversation, certain the thunderclap had revealed my true location. Trek would have listened to my background noise just as I had listened to his, but even if he knew I was in our neighborhood, would he suspect that I would be brazen enough to steal into his house again? I thought of the weapons stored in the closet under the stairs and broke into a run, the flutter of sheet lightning guiding me down the street.

By the time I reached Trek's house, people had begun setting out candles and hurricane lanterns, but no light glimmered in his windows. I glanced in the garage. The Mercedes was gone. Maybe Trek was already waiting for me near Tulley's, intent on catching me the moment I arrived.

I turned off my phone ringer, the sky ablaze with lightning. While thunder shook the house, I tried the back door. Left unlocked, either carelessly or purposefully, it swung open. The effortless way I had broken in caused doubt to worm into my thoughts. More cautious now, fearful that I had walked into a trap, I crossed the back porch, opened the door to the kitchen, and eased into deeper shadows.

The linoleum creaked beneath my feet and, immediately, Pixie and Bonnie began barking. Shut inside the laundry room, they scratched at the closed door. Had Trek penned them in the room to keep them out of his way? If he was in the house and not waiting near Tulley's as I supposed, then the dogs had alerted him to my arrival.

I sensed movement and hunkered down as the laundry room

259

door burst open. Pixie and Bonnie raced toward me, mewling. I tried to calm them, brushing my hands over their wet snouts, my concentration on the dark behind them. Had someone opened the door for them, or had an old latch given way to the persistent beating from their paws?

With the dogs licking my face, I cupped my hand around my cell phone, scrolled down to Satch's number, and pressed Send. If Trek still had Satch's phone, the ringtone might give me his location. When I heard only the ringing in my earpiece, I ended the call, confident that Trek wasn't near. He could still be upstairs, or perhaps, like me, he had turned off his ringtone, but even if he had, he would have checked the caller ID and, in the dark, the display glow would have given his presence away. For the moment, I felt safe enough to stand.

I pulled out the bag of dog food from under the kitchen sink and dropped it open on the floor. Kibble scattered across the linoleum, the meaty smell rising in the clammy air. Pixie and Bonnie ate, chuffing and snorting. Now that their barking had stopped, I heard the wind chimes. Someone must have left a window open. The loud clattering would camouflage the sound of anyone sneaking up on me while I searched for Satch in the bedrooms and attic.

Intent on stopping the noise, I opened the drawer near the stove and drew out the scissors. I slipped them in my pocket, blades pointed down, and stole forward through the dining room and into the living room, where I entered the closet under the stairs.

The smell of gun cleaner sunk deep into the back of my nose, the harsh scent leaving a bitter taste on my tongue. I glided my hand over the empty nails, surprised that so many guns were missing. For a moment, I panicked, fearing Dante had removed all of them, and then my fingers swept over three guns that hung upside down, their trigger guards hooked over nails. I chose the one whose weight assured me that it had the power to kill.

After testing the balance, my fingers worked over the gun to make sure it was loaded. I clicked off the safety and eased back into the living room as a car drove past the house. The beam from the headlights swept across the walls. A man-size shadow stood near the TV, a gun aimed at me. I fell to the floor, the point of the scissors digging into my thigh, and held my gun with both hands, then stared at the dark, waiting for a muzzle flash and an explosion of bullets.

When lightning lit the room again, the phantom shadow had disappeared. Even so, for one horrible moment, I wondered if Trek was following me, ghoulishly waiting for me to discover Satch's body. I listened for his footsteps, a sigh of breath, but the wind chimes made it impossible to hear anything other than thunder. I waited for another lightning strike.

The eerie glow burst across the night, lighting the room, and proved to me that I was alone. Relief and bewilderment flooded through me. The spectral figure must have been an illusion, a trick of light and shadow and my nerves.

I stood and edged up the steps, my back pressed against the wall, the wind chimes unsettling me as much as my inability to see. I had almost reached the landing when Pixie and Bonnie, finished with eating, bounded up after me. They whimpered, nosing my legs, their bodies shivering—from cold or fear?—and continued up with me.

In the upstairs hallway, I set the gun down, then took out the scissors and cut the strings that moored the wind chimes to the railing. Seashells, glass cutouts, and metal tubes fell into the blackness below. When only strings glided over my fingers, I listened to the wind-thrashed trees brushing against the house, the rain clicking at the windows. Though I heard no sound of another person, something felt wrong.

After a moment, I realized that the dogs were no longer with me. Their sudden disappearance nagged at me, but I didn't have time to search for them. I needed to find Satch. I picked up the gun as lightning zipped across the sky, its pale light stuttering into the hallway. When thunder pealed, I heard a yelp, cut off midway through the cry. I froze, listening, terror becoming an icy pit in my stomach.

In the silence that followed, a whisper of stealthy footsteps came from downstairs. The front door opened, then slammed with a bang that rattled the house. I hurried to Trek's bedroom window and looked down at the street.

His Mercedes was parked at the curb, the dome light on, headlights beaming. Trek sat behind the steering wheel, his hair shaved off in a neat square above his temple, where a row of butterfly stitches pinched his swollen scalp.

While he gazed back at the house from the open car window, I calculated the angle, the line of fire, and saw my opportunity: the perfect shot from the front door.

I took off and rushed blindly down the stairs, seashells and glass crunching under my shoes. I had almost reached the bottom when I stepped on something soft and slipped. I lost my balance and tumbled down, landing flat on the floor, my concentration on holding the gun barrel pointed away from me.

I sat up and, with pain still rotating in my neck, used the display light on my cell phone to see what had tripped me. A cry escaped my lungs. Bonnie lay on the floor, pink belly up, forepaws splayed, with Pixie, not moving, on the step above her. I dropped the gun and phone and picked up Bonnie, cradling her still-warm body against my chest. Her head lolled to the side, her neck broken.

My tears came with great leaping sobs.

The phone vibrated. I glanced at it, buzzing on the rug. The caller ID read "Satch." I set Bonnie down and grabbed the phone, grief intensifying my rage.

"You killed your own dogs!" I yelled. "What did they do that you had to kill them?"

"It's your fault, Blaise," Trek said smoothly. "The dogs wouldn't be dead if you'd kept your promise. We agreed on a trade, and I've been watching you creep around my house with one of my own guns like you thought I was fool enough to let you shoot me again."

"Where's Satch?" My throat burned with hatred, though my body felt stone cold.

"Can you taste the adrenaline yet?" Trek asked in reply to my question. "Does it make you feel out of control or just scared?"

"Let Satch go," I said, keeping my voice even, "and I'll come to you."

"What makes you think he's still alive?" Trek asked.

I hurled the phone across the room, then, swooping up the gun, jumped to my feet and opened the front door. The car had gone dark and was rolling away, my chance lost. Trek had made himself the perfect target for a front door shot only to lure me down the stairs at breakneck speed so I would trip over the dogs.

When lightning illuminated the car, I aimed for the back windshield and pulled the trigger. The gun choked. The firing pin had been removed, an easy trick. Trek had known all along that I would break into his house in an attempt to save Satch, and had left only defective weapons in the closet.

Anger ripped through my adrenaline-soaked body. Trek assumed I would die like the terrorized bull in the fighting ring. He had forgotten that sometimes the mortally wounded bull gored the matador.

With cold rain slapping my face, I stood across the street from Trek's house, feeling unbelievably tired and tense with worry. Where was Satch? I had searched the upstairs rooms and attic, using the blazing bristles of a broom for my torchlight, and hadn't found him. Tomorrow, with sunlight to guide me, I would begin another search. This one in the Borderlands, which offered a thousand places to hide someone.

Trek's earlier call, with the background noise of wind chimes, had been purposeful, to draw me here. I had a strong, intuitive feeling that he had something more planned, but before I could face him again, I had to get some sleep. I knew one place where I'd be welcome if I was caught breaking inside.

With thunder rumbling around me, I picked up my purse and made my way to Orchid Terrace. By the time I entered the lobby, I was shaking. Emergency lamps set in the wall sent shafts of light down the long corridor, which smelled of insect spray and urine. The only decor came from a child's scribbling, a snarl of green and purple crayon lines trailing knee-high down to Kaylee's apartment, where she and her sisters would be sleeping.

Using the key I found hidden on the backside of her doormat, I quietly let myself in and listened. Everyone seemed to be in bed. I peeled off my drenched clothing, then took the nightgown from my purse and slipped it over my head.

A strange fear came over me. Realistically, I knew I couldn't feel Trek looking for me, and yet, I did. Without making a sound, I crossed to the window and peered out, past the rain ticking against the glass. I had expected to see the Mercedes parked on the street with Trek smiling up at me and, though I saw only darkness, my apprehension didn't go away. I had the uncomfortable sense that Trek was gazing out at the night to where I stood.

To calm my fear, I searched the kitchen for a weapon, my hands grazing over utensils until I touched a knife with an unusual curve and sharpness. I set it on the coffee table within easy reach, then curled onto the couch, my mind going back and forth between sleep and wakefulness, as my worries dissolved into dreams.

Sometime later, I awakened to the murmur of rain and wind and knew instinctively that another sound had invaded my sleep and roused me. Through half-opened eyes, I watched the darkness glide around me and, though I saw no shadow deeper than the others, I eased my hand across the coffee table, my fingers grasping for the knife. *Where was it?*

A hand caught my wrist.

"Is this what you were looking for?" The knife nicked my cheek, the curved tip hooking on flesh as the blade tore free. "Crazy girl," Trek said, his voice barely audible. "Did you think you could use this on me?"

I didn't move, or even reply, because energy emanated off Trek, a heat I could feel. Any show of fear or panic could excite him and cause him to lose his remaining self-restraint.

"There won't be any more fooling around." His words, carried on hushed breath, grazed over my face. "We're going out to the car, and if you wake Kaylee or one of her sisters, I'll kill them all. If you try to run, I'll come back and—"

I nodded my intention to cooperate, grateful he wasn't going to butcher me here and leave my corpse for Kaylee and her sisters to find in the morning. Soundlessly, I made my way across the room and into the hallway, conscious of Trek behind me, the knife against my back. The tip bore through the nightgown, into my skin, pressing in and out with the rhythm of my steps, more stinging annoyance than pain, but holding the promise of Trek's readiness to drive the blade between my ribs and into my heart.

I waded through the gutter to the Mercedes, which idled at the curb, the engine chuffing softly. Trek opened the car door, his gaze riveted on me, oblivious to the rain that struck his face. My survival instinct told me to ram my head into his jaw, rake my fingernails down his scalp, tear out the stitches, and flee. But unbidden came the images of Kaylee and her sisters dead, and my knees gave way. I fell into the passenger seat.

Grinning, satisfied that I wasn't going to bolt, Trek slammed the car door, walked around to the driver's side, and slid behind the steering wheel. The windshield wipers began a quiet, rhythmic sweep as he shifted into gear and the car rolled forward, the street lit with gray light reflected off the clouds.

I took slow, deep breaths to keep my mind from fleeing into panic and stared at the row houses, shrouded behind windswept sheets of rain. As terrible as my life had been in this neighborhood, I yearned for it now, but I couldn't let Kaylee and her sisters die in my stead.

A few blocks later, the car swerved over to the curb in front of Trek's house. I had assumed that he had been taking me to the Borderlands, where he could hide my body. That he would risk killing me inside his home unsettled me, though why one place should feel worse for dying than another should, I didn't understand.

Trek opened the car door and, using the knife as a pointer, motioned me onto the walk and up to the front door. I stepped inside, stunned to see candles, dozens and dozens of flickering flames, that lined the hallway down to the back porch. Someone had cleared the broken wind chimes off the stairs, the kibble from the kitchen floor.

"I guess Melissa has already started cleaning up," I said, wondering what had been done with Pixie and Bonnie.

"Forget Melissa. I told you she means nothing to me." He pointed the knife toward the stairs and I began my march.

In his bedroom, more candles lined the floor and windows, wax pooling on the floorboards and dripping craggy lines from the sills. I had not expected to die quickly, or painlessly, but so many candles implied ritual, torture, a brutal death. I scanned the room for anything I could use as a weapon. A glass ashtray sat on the dresser beneath red tapers that wept wax onto the wood.

Trek pulled off his soggy shirt and tossed it aside. An Egyptian ankh dangled from a chain around his neck.

"That's Danny's!" My mind swirled through all the possible ways Trek might have gotten it.

"Mine now." He laughed. "Danny wasn't even unconscious when the three of you walked away from him. I had to finish the job I'd sent you to do. I only let him live because he loves Ariel." Trek smiled at the shock on my face. "While I beat him, I told him that I'd kill her if he ever got near her again. Just one hello and she'd be dead."

Rage seized me. I grabbed the ashtray and lunged at Trek, intent on shattering it against his eye.

He swung up. The knife slashed the underside of my arm, cutting through skin and muscle until the blade scraped bone. My arm fell useless at my side, the ashtray bouncing across the floor. Fierce pain throbbed through me, but the straight cut barely bled.

"The game's over," Trek said as he stroked the knife across my shoulder. The blade snagged on the strap of my nightgown and, with a quick snap of his wrist, Trek cut through it.

At last, I understood the reason Trek had taken me to his home and not the Borderlands. I had prepared myself for death, for pain, but not this. Shaking my head, I backed away.

"There's something you should know," Trek said softly,

leaning closer, his hair dripping water onto my skin. "In case you were wondering, I didn't kill Satch."

"Satch," I breathed. "Where is he?"

"In the Borderlands," Trek whispered, "stashed away. He's sly like his dad. It took me almost the whole day to catch him, but I like the game. Now I got him all cozy, coiled up in barbed wire, a feast for the rats, unless someone frees him."

Lightheaded from the pain tearing through my arm, I stared at Trek, trying to detect a lie, and found nothing to indicate that he wasn't speaking the truth.

"If you stop pretending like you don't want me," Trek continued. "I'll let you cut the barbed wire that's holding him. But if you want him dead—"

"Free him," I whispered.

Trek searched my eyes, looking for an answer deeper than my words had given him. He tossed the knife onto the bed and embraced me, careful of my wounded arm. "You'll learn to love me," he said, his lips moving tenderly against my forehead.

A terrible stillness came over me. My legs, which had been trembling, stopped shaking. *I can survive this. I can survive.* And when this was over, if I was alive, I was going to the police.

Snitches get stitches, my mind warned automatically. A snitch was despised. A snitch was a target. A snitch had to run for her life or be killed. *So what?* I thought. Anything is better than living this way.

After . . . after . . . after . . . I promised myself as a glint of steel flashed in my side vision. Something cracked against my skull and sent numbing pain down my spine. I fell on my back, scattering a line of candles. Flames, skating over the spilled wax, sputtered toward me as wisps of black smoke curled into my eyes.

Breathless, berating myself for letting my guard down, I rolled over to escape Trek's next blow and knocked against him. He lay on the floor beside me, facedown, a gash bleeding on the side of his head.

38

Through my pulsing vision, Melissa came into focus, leaning over Trek, a tire iron clutched in her hand, her face contorted with terror for what she had done—for what she was about to do.

"I don't care if I have to spend the rest of my life in jail," she said. "I'm taking my freedom back."

In spite of the pain shrieking through my head and arm, I managed to stand and fall against her in time to block her swing. "You don't need to kill him." With my good hand, I loosened her grip until the tire iron slipped free and hit the floor with a dull thunk. "We'll get him another way," I said, my voice choking on tears of relief, anger, and pain.

Her fingers touched my scalp, blood from the wound running in tiny rivulets over her hand. "I didn't mean to hit you. I only wanted to stop Trek. There was no way I was going to let him hurt you."

"How did you know I needed help?" I asked, collapsing on the edge of the bed.

"Kaylee." Melissa picked up the corner of the sheet. I flinched when she pressed it against my head to stop the bleeding. "She woke up a little while ago and found her front door open, blood on her couch, and your purse on the floor. She called me and I came here as fast as I could."

I squeezed her hand in gratitude. "Give me your phone," I said. "I need to call the cops."

Melissa laughed nervously. "You're going to snitch?" She took Trek's cell phone from his pocket and handed it to me, her fingers trembling.

"You don't need to stay," I said, fighting to remain conscious as I propped the phone on my lap. With my working hand, I tapped in three numbers and pressed Send. "I can stand against Trek alone."

"I've got secrets that will put him in prison for sixty years." After examining the slash on my head, Melissa added, "Tell them to send an ambulance, too."

By the time I had finished my 911 call, I was slumped against Melissa, my blood soaking into her clothes, her sobs convulsing through me as I drifted in and out of consciousness.

"Everything's going to be all right." I tried to soothe her, though I couldn't stop my own worry about Satch. I imagined him bound and slowly starving to death. "Don't cry," I added as my tears fell.

I heard my name called out and struggled to turn my head. Satch crossed the room, his arms gouged and trailing blood from the cuts where rusted spurs had dug into his skin.

"Satch," I whispered, joy rising inside me.

He kneeled in front of me, unable to hide his fear. "I thought you'd run away, but Trek told me you'd come back. Then he told me what he was going to do to you. I tried to get here sooner." He glanced at Trek, who lay unconscious on the floor.

"I did it," Melissa said. "And accidentally hit Blaise, too."

Satch grasped my hand as my eyes started to close. "Stay with me, Toughness. Come on."

I nodded but could no longer fight the darkness. I gave in to its peace, the irresistible currents that pulled me back to the memories of my childhood, when I still believed that I could live my life in a bold and powerful way without a gun.

But as I spiraled down, I thought of the little kids in my neighborhood who saw gangsters and drug dealers on their way to school, and suddenly I imagined a different future. Struggling, I fought through the layers of consciousness until I came back and opened my eyes, my chest heaving as I took in air, my pain unbearable.

"Help's on the way," Satch said, lifting me, unaware of the wound under my arm. I winced at the sudden sting before warm blood flowed over my side.

Sirens shrilled, growing louder, as Satch carried me down the stairs and outside into the cold, Melissa beside us.

Two squad cars turned the corner, their lights flashing across the puddles left from the rain. An ambulance sped behind them.

"I think I've been looking at life the wrong way," I said. "Maybe when fate gives you something bad, it's not to defeat you, it's so you'll see the problem and do something about it."

"I took care of my problem," Melissa said with a sad laugh before she grabbed my hand, trying to calm her nerves.

"Well," Satch whispered as the officers stepped out of their cars and approached us warily. "Are you ready for this?"

"No," I said. "But I'm going to do it anyway."